BANK NOTES

To Steven

Best Wishes

Will

Also by Will Nett

My Only Boro: A Walk Through Red & White

Billy No Maps: Teessider on Tour

Local Author Writes Book

The Golfer's Lament: How I Reached For The Pars...
And Missed

Find Will Nett on twitter at: will_nett

BANK NOTES

WILL NETT

Published in paperback in 2021 by Sixth Element Publishing on behalf of Will Nett.

by Sixth Element Publishing
Arthur Robinson House
13-14 The Green
Billingham TS23 1EU
www.6epublishing.net

© Will Nett 2021

ISBN 978-1-914170-19-5

British Library Cataloguing in Publication Data. A catalogue record for this book is available from the British Library.

All rights reserved. No part of this publication may be reproduced, stored in a retrieval system or transmitted, in any form or by any means, electronic, mechanical, photocopying, recording and/or otherwise without the prior written permission of the publishers. This book may not be lent, resold, hired out or disposed of by way of trade in any form, binding or cover other than that in which it is published without the prior written consent of the publishers.

Will Nett asserts the moral right to be identified as the author of this work.

Printed in Great Britain.

CONTENTS

Introduction 1
The Médecin Men 3
The Unwelcome Guest 17
The Tunley Hum 45
Come to Kepler 59
Goin' Back to Prestwick 85
The Devil and the Farmer 89
The Headhunters 98
The Anfield Murder 107
The Cat and the Cake Tin 114
The Bergstrom Case 124

INTRODUCTION

For some time now, I've wanted to write a collection of short stories, and bring together a handful of existing ones. As I approached the 10th anniversary of the publication of my first book, I also wanted to create something in the vein of the anthologies and authors, filmmakers and artists that have inspired my own work. This collection is as much influenced by Round The Twist, Tales of the Unexpected, and The Twilight Zone, for example, as it is by Robert Aickman, Shirley Jackson and Stephen King. In fact, like many of the stories you are about to read, the lines between film, TV, literature, and, indeed, real life, are often blurred, and here are stirred into a curious melting pot of mystery, occasional malevolence, and detached body parts. The collection, though, is not without the humour of my previous non-fiction work, as followers will see within the opening story. The sharp-eyed amongst you may notice recurring themes throughout. As many of the stories were written at different stages of the past decade, this is more likely a result of my sub-conscious bleeding into the work, than any deliberate attempts to link them together.

Many of the characters that you are about to be introduced to may well be known to you, in some distant capacity, as will the events described, some of which I myself became embroiled in, others less so, but, as always, I leave it up to the reader to decide which.

THE MEDÉCIN MEN

Just over twenty years ago, I went to Nice and rented what would be best described as a garret, over Rue Droite, a few streets back from the famous promenade, away from the broiling nouveau-riche holidaymakers that travelled down on what is still occasionally referred to as the 'Blue Train' route, from Paris, and London. The novelty of the romantic squalor of French novels and arthouse cinema depictions soon wore off, as did the tuneless daily balcony performance from the budding Argentinian opera singer in the next room. Her enthusiasm, though, was admirable, and not even dimmed when the old woman living above us, on one occasion, emptied a tureen of cold water over her. The old crone scored a double-hit as most of the excess water ran off the canopy of the florists below, and soaked the shoeless gypsy kids that spent much of their days making a racket and pickpocketing tourists.

I hoped to do something similar on a grander scale, and with less noise. The room was a cold-water set-up with a single bed barely big enough to sleep one, and a bay window of sorts that housed an entire eco-system of rent-dodging flies and spiders. Eventually, I found a job on a building site over in Caucade, a few miles out of the city centre. The cool winds blowing through the airport flight paths from the south west of the city made the temperatures a lot more bearable for a *fantôme* like me. I was 'le fantôme' amongst my new co-workers, on account of my deathly pallor, which was even more pronounced alongside the proliferation of bronzed locals and African migrant workers. The work didn't pay much but after a few weeks I was in good physical shape and rapidly developing my French, largely in the form of insults. My new vocabulary further expanded over our regular Friday card game, in the back room of the Red Fox pub, or Le Reynard Roux, to give it its local name.

"It not 'Red Fox'," Chelou would always say to me, "c'est le 'Reynard Roux'," exaggerating his French accent. Chelou was a big Niçois, the go-to man on the site amongst the lower-caste of the hierarchy that I was now part of. He had a big round head that carried an analytical brain, and shoulders like cantaloupe melons, but was softly spoken with it. That round head was full of figures. He had a real knack for distances and measurements. You could almost see his mind weighing things up: hands of cards, personalities. He never bluffed at poker, which by definition meant you could often predict his hand. Instead, he'd calculate carefully, at odds with my own approach of chaotic blagging, an opposite reaction, perhaps, to my non-poker playing conservatism. He would count a stack of bricks at a glance, or measure a piece of wood the same, all skills he eventually decided to turn to something considerably more profitable. We were breaking a tartine together on the site one day when he asked me if I ever went swimming off the Plage Beau Rivage. He was asking as a local, who wouldn't be seen dead in tourist areas like that particular stretch of beach. He still considered me a tourist, even though I'd been there for around six months by then. Other than visiting the casinos on the Promenade des Anglais, and the occasional supper at Le Chantecler to impress a date that I certainly couldn't afford, I rarely visited the beach. The novelty had long worn off and I've never been a sun-worshipper.

"You know the Paillon, Guillame?" he asked, using the French version of my name. This seemed to denote that we were officially *amis*. He always called me *fantôme* in front of the others.

I knew the prom de Paillon, the street that cuts across Place Masséna. It's a large civic space with the Fontaine du Soleil as its centrepiece.

He was referring to the Paillon itself, a huge open sewer that bisects the city along the Avenue Jean Medécin, and runs out into the sea. It was effectively a dry sewer, dispensing a mere trickle for the most part, and otherwise serving as a drainage route for flooding, which is rare in Nice.

I gave a hugely over-exaggerated Gallic shrug, that only an Englishman could produce, as Chelou bit further into his bread.

"Runs all the way to foothills under the Peripherique," he said, waving to the north of the city.

"So fuck," I replied, busting through another piece of tooth-shattering bread.

"All the way to beach," he continued. He was driving at something, in his usual analytical way. "Through Avenue Jean Medécin. Under la banque," he said. He left the sentence hanging in the air and swept a streak of breadcrumbs from his t-shirt. "For the rats," he said, heaving himself up. "Interesting creature, this rat, Guillame. Everything it need, in sewer." He belched, and strode off.

That night I got off the bus on the promenade behind the Opera House and walked back on myself towards the underground carpark entrance at Rue Sulzer. You can still walk right beneath the city by accessing via the Paillon.

Chelou and I talked some more, over the following weeks. He told me that his older sister had worked at the bank a few years earlier. He remembered one particular occasion, following a flood in the building next door, and how the damaged flooring led straight into the Paillon beneath. Only the bank knew about it and had kept it to themselves for security purposes, but more likely due to them apparently having no adequate insurance cover. Throughout the 1970s and 80s, under the Mayorship of Jacques Medécin, Nice was a cesspit of corporate corruption so a bank with no insurance during that period was not as strange as it may seem. Chelou pressed me on the job, tentatively, or as tentatively as a Frenchman could press.

"Everything we need is here," he said, enthusiastically. He was right.

I began to make a mental inventory of required

equipment. Chelou had almost certainly done the same, with much greater accuracy and detail. You could drive a fair-sized vehicle, a van, I thought, into the entrance at Rue Sulzer, and probably further. We did a recce on foot one Monday night, slipping unnoticed into the opening at the sea wall. I carried a torch as Chelou noted in his head where each building above us should be. As he did so, I chalked on the walls the buildings that corresponded to Chelou's mind map. The sewer was widest beneath the Fontaine du Soleil, as we expected, but there were no obvious signs of anyone having been there for some time. I chalked off Avenue de Verdun, Rue Gioffredo and Galleries Lafayette as we crept through the city towards the bank. The water was little more than a dribble; easily avoidable in the dryness of the summer months. Eventually, we reached the bank. We had no floor plan as yet but we at least knew we were in the vicinity. Chelou gave the tunnel sides a firm whack with his hand, then took a small claw hammer and chisel from his pocket and scraped away a small piece of stone from the wall. He fingered it carefully, sifting the spoil. Then he slid what was left into his pocket. He opened a nearby run-off drain cover and placed the hammer and chisel carefully into the trickling stream, wrapped in a plastic bag.

He didn't say anything the whole way back.

Gradually, we put it together in more detail. I considered it low risk. We could work quietly, or relatively so, without being disturbed but we would need more muscle for the heavy work. Chelou predicted there would be no less than eight metres of reasonably soft stone to drill through before we reached the vault. A four-man team; he had another two men in mind. A pair of ex-Legionnaire brothers, both apparently called Daniel, would alternate working with us in four hour spells, every Saturday night for three months, August through November, giving us around two hundred and fifty man hours to infiltrate the vault. We would then raid the vault itself, at our leisure, over the Millennium holiday.

Over the course of three months, we drilled and chipped our way to the vault, boring out a 10ft wide hole that we strengthened with boarding and support joists every three metres. The Two Daniels were typical Legionnaires, tacit and ineloquent, but industrious. Serious. I still don't know their real names. The likelihood of two brothers both being called Daniel seemed low. Chelou was always vouching for them, which made me even more suspicious of them. We'd played cards a few times and been for an occasional drink. My general view was that anyone who tipped out in Nice, connected with the Legion, was either on the run from it, or on the run to it. Previously they'd been stationed in Papeete, Tahiti, where they'd run a semi-successful racket making and importing false teeth to sell to other Legionnaires, who would then present them to their ever-grateful Tahitian mistresses. Indian Givers to the last, they would take the teeth back when they went on tour so the women would be less likely to attract potential husbands in their absence. Now they were drilling away at a different kind of project.

Dan Une, as I called him, was a thin-lipped Berber from Siddi Bel Abbès, the older of the two. Dan Deux was born a year or two after his brother, to a different mother, in Nice. Dan Une ribbed his brother about his lack of Algerian heritage, knowing that he hated the French, a hangover from the War of Independence that their parents had lived through, but was officially a Frenchman. Like many young brothers, they produced a constant friction that looked like it would culminate in a will to fight each other to the death at a moment's notice. They were in it for paper money but I envisaged them being overwhelmed by jewels and the like and trying to take more than they could ever have use for. It never really occurred to me that we were about to commit an act of unchecked stupidity, or remarkable boldness, depending on how it turned it out. An act that, if it went wrong, could see me, us, jailed for a very long time. I was still a teenager. I could end up in a French jail until long after my fortieth birthday.

It felt like a game, a bit of fun, maybe because we felt we could never be caught.

The mood as we worked away was relaxed; we felt untouchable, but that's when mistakes occur. That was always in the back of my mind but I put it aside and kept on drilling, and ploughing, and digging. The sweat squirted out of me and cooled in the autumn air. With that, and the day job, I was reduced to almost skeletal form. I'm a thin man to begin with. By the time Christmas arrived, I was turning to dust. Chelou had slipped around 50lbs and the Two Daniel's were no more than streaks of raw-steak eating sinew after years on a Foreign Legion diet of jam, bread, and black coffee. It became a running joke that we could have saved ourselves a lot of hassle digging and instead just post me through the letterbox at the front door of the bank.

We wore the clichéd apparel of the criminal gang: boiler suits, hard hats and hi-viz vests that I'd stolen from another building site over in Saint-Andrieu. It might have thrown the scent off, if we were sighted; the idea being that four men working in a sewer would not have looked especially suspicious. I packed a holdall, as I had done every weekend for most of the previous six months of the 20th century, for the final time, on the morning of New Year's Eve 1999, as the fêtes nationales got underway on the Place Masséna. We agreed to take away no more, not even a single franc, than we could fit in each of our holdalls. No bundles of notes or gold chains slipping out of the side pockets. I suspected there would be exceptions to the rule. I packed in a set of waterproofs – it had been a damp Christmas – the helmet and head torch, and several pairs of gloves, surgical and leather. I hadn't worn gloves at all during the groundwork. It occurred to me that I was trying to prove my 'working man' credentials to Chelou. A crowbar, a 10lb hammer, three chisels of varying size, spare torch batteries, and a bottle of red from Chateau de Bellet, up north where I'd taken a vineyard tour when I first arrived in the country.

"Bring bouteille," Chelou had said. "We make weekend."

What the fuck did I think I was doing? In a few hours, I would take the pistol I kept taped to the bottom of a floorboard, stuff it in my sock, pick up the holdall and stride through the Old Town, never to return.

We expected the vault to be well stocked with paper money. There'd been a lot of noise over the previous few years about the French converting to the euro. As a result, the ever-jittery Niçoise and exiled Monagasques had started frantically dumping money into accounts with a view to keeping it safe and eventually transferring it to fuck-knows-where, most likely a few miles along the coast to the tax-free Utopia of Monaco. As it transpired, half a billion francs-worth of euros remain unchanged over twenty years later, and have since been recorded as revenue by the government. We were hoping to make a minor dent in it but we were all looking for different things. I set myself a cash limit of 200,000 francs, an amount I knew I could comfortably salt away without too much difficulty until things settled down, but what I really wanted was watches. I had some precise models in mind, or at least pieces like them, that I felt we would discover, based on some loose intelligence gathered from a dealer I knew in Geneva. We couldn't be 100% certain of the contents, of course; every box could turn out to be empty, but the dealer, who I'm still in touch with, traded regularly with the Niçoise elite. He couldn't know which banks they used, but I was ready to take my chance in the pile.

It was agreed that myself and the Two Dans would alternate over the three nights as street level lookouts, based on the Esplanade Georges Pompidou, in a fake removals van emblazoned with 'N et N Deplacement', our fledgling new business venture that would exist for no longer than four days. We'd tried our lookout routine a few times without any issues.

Inside the van I'd laid on the fold out bed, reading August Le Breton's *Du Rififi Chez Les Hommes* with a walkie talkie on my chest but was rarely disturbed by anything I needed to bring to the attention of the others. There was nothing going on, even over the weekends, other than the usual string of Saturday night revellers, stumbling to and from casinos with unaffordable Russian prostitutes hanging off their necks, teenagers vomiting on each other, and the occasional police car.

Fittingly, it was Chelou who made the push that took us through to the vault two weeks earlier, the white hot drill bit that we'd doused with gallons of water throughout the year jarring to a halt against the back of what we suspected was a wall of safe deposit boxes.

Chelou threw down the drill and Dan Deux pushed between the pair of us and fell upon the tiny opening like a dying man in the desert falling on a watering hole.

"Cul sec," I cried, nodding at Chelou as I threw off my ear protectors that by now had pooled with sweat and cement dust. *Dry arse*, that classic French compliment when someone pulls off something impressive.

Dan Deux burst into hysterical laughter, like a comic

book villain, further highlighting what I thought was an ever-worsening instability. Dan Une gave a reserved thumbs-up, by contrast, from the back of the group as he leaned on the shovel that had been throwing back the spoil.

There was still plenty to do. We needed to make the hole big enough for Chelou, easily the broadest of us all, to fit through, but we were flying close to the sun now. We'd been drilling for less than an hour on that occasion but we stopped the job right there for a fortnight in order to plan the actual breakthrough, now we knew what we were dealing with. We tidied out the passage of all debris, boarded out the distance we had dug that night, put in two more support joists, and scuttled off back towards the Promenade.

The beachfront fireworks had long started by the time we fully punched through the wall on that New Year's Eve, and made enough space behind the boxes to squeeze in. There was none of the joy I anticipated after months of work, more a quiet amazement that we'd managed to get in there at all, and a dawning realisation that we were going ahead with it. We dragged ourselves up through the hole, elbowing and scratching our way through the damaged edges of the wall, with Chelou leading the way. Dan Deux, ahead of me, was next in, rolling over on to his back and the floor of the vault as my head popped through the hole. I dragged the bags in after me.

"Ua here vau ia oe," he cried, heaving himself off the

floor. *Ua here vau ia oe.* Tahitian, I presumed. He grabbed Chelou's big cold-sweat coated head between his hands and pulled it towards him. "Ua here vau ia oe," he said again, louder, kissing Chelou's head.

"Ssssh," said Chelou, pushing him away. "Silence."

There was an almost ceremonial beginning to the box openings, led by Chelou. It was an unspoken custom that the mastermind, *le chef*, opened proceedings… the digging of the first sod, the champagne bottle against the boat hull. The Two Daniels and I stood in a loose triangle in the centre of the room as Chelou took to his wall. We agreed to work one each of the four walls that held the boxes, with the fourth man still on look out. We had selected our walls at random using highest card draw. This way there was no suggestion of anyone interfering with anyone else's haul, or any benefit to knowing what might be in a particular box via any perceived tip-offs. I drew the wall with the door in it. Less boxes. Chelou looked for a reaction. I said nothing but it showed me that that if it was him, he wouldn't have been happy about it.

I pulled a five of clubs on the lookout draw, Chelou… an Ace, and Dan Deux… a queen of hearts. Dan Une's three of clubs put him on first watch. We rotated watch out of fairness to each man, and on the reasoning that four different faces, if noticed, would be harder to identify individually by potential witnesses. Chelou struggled ungainly with that first box, his energy sapped by the climb through the hole, and the contents – the deeds to some French property – deflated him. Where was the good stuff?

"À la mur, chaque," I said. *Each to their wall.*

I speared my crowbar into the base of one of the boxes with a mighty blow I didn't know I had in me. It juddered against the metal, sparking against the clasp, which broke clean off as the bar flew from my hands. A fluke, but one that was good for morale.

Chelou stepped forward, began to reach out.

"Aie, aie," I shouted, "c'est a moi."

I pulled the damaged drawer out carefully with the tip of a chisel. It was full of jewellery. Chelou's heavy jaw swung low as I raked the chisel through an octopus of gold chain, sparkling bracelets and necklaces. Emeralds, rubies and diamonds spilled from the drawer and spattered over the floor like hailstones.

Without even drawing a line on his target, Dan Deux thundered his bar at a random box, and so began forty-five minutes of almost orgiastic 'box-popping', as we called it, that engulfed the three of us whole. I fell away in exhaustion, the loot piled up to my shinbones. A swamp of wealth dragging us into its fevered heart. Dan Deux was down to his underwear in the heat, despite the time of year, and wearing a jewel encrusted tiara that he'd prised free of its box.

"La Roi de Nice," I said, as Chelou turned and broke into laughter.

"La Roi du Monde," he said. *King of the World.*

I haven't seen Chelou, or the Two Dans, since we walked out of the tunnel in the nascent days of the new Millennium. I haven't looked for them, nor they for me, presumably. The police investigation into the job is still open, as far as I'm aware, over twenty years later. I think about it, sometimes, whenever I'm back in Nice, maybe once a year, sunbathing on my preferred patch of Beau Rivage beach in the shadow of the Neuf Lignes Obliques sculpture.

THE UNWELCOME GUEST

Gedeon rolled over and embraced his wife from behind. She murmured as he smiled to himself and allowed the tips of her glistening black hair to tickle the end of his nose. He refused to open his eyes, knowing he would have to surrender to waking. He closed them tighter, before finally succumbing, and squinted at the face of his watch. His biological alarm had activated long before the bedside clock had even thought about chiming. He smiled at the irony of it, but there was no question of him oversleeping today. He pulled away the covers, taking a moment to gaze upon Daeza's dark, slender figure, before walking off some of his early-morning rigidity in the direction of the window.

He watched the crane operators as they removed the huge icicles that clung to the apartment ledges along his street, a familiar sight during Krakowian winters. Further across Krasinskiego he saw mounds of compacted black snow piled high, as the chill of the condensation clung to his naked body. He felt it around his waist and on his chest as he stepped back, and began to remove his watch. He turned the face over and studied the inscription: *Daeza Na Wieki Wieków. For All Eternity.*

Gedeon didn't wear it for work, and now placed it

carefully on the bedside table, alongside his wedding ring, taking care not to disturb his wife. His bones began to loosen as he entered the bathroom, but again grew tense at the touch of his bare feet on the cold tiles. He studied his reflection, the image and the person within, thinking about the waiting day's work, as he filled the basin with cold water and trailed his razorblade through the eddies.

He rinsed his face and returned to the bedroom. He opened the wardrobe and carefully removed the clothes he'd prepared yesterday, lifting them by the hangers well clear of the floor, and placing them into an adjoining room. He closed the door behind him and again looked at himself, this time in the room's full-length mirror. He was satisfied. No excess bodyweight, instead a lean 6 foot tall frame that would soon satisfy the hunger it had cultivated. He dressed slowly and deliberately, beginning with the disagreeably expensive underwear Daeza had bought him, seemingly for her own benefit. He pulled on his trousers and began to feel ready. He savoured the tailoring of a bespoke, ice blue Tovsky Brothers' shirt as it touched against his skin.

Not easily swayed by persuasive salesmen, he had bought a matching tie and a sword motif tie-pin to complement the shirt. As a rule, it was always socks and shoes last. He cringed slightly, as he slid into a pair of black leather moccasins, at the thought of the potential damage from the weather conditions but they were his only option today. He needed to move his feet quietly, comfortably, and quickly. He took one final look in the mirror, inspecting his body armour, and again liked what he saw, and headed silently down the stairs.

In the kitchen, he removed a tea towel from the back of the door and laid it out neatly in front of the oven. Then he slowly lowered onto his knees, firmly fixing his hands on either side of the oven door. With all his strength, he heaved it out of its recess. He moved the tea towel, laying it in the newly-created space behind the oven, and crawled into the gap. It was too dark to see anything but he did not require any light. He had done it many times before, his muscle memory allowing him to feel instinctively for the sunken floorboard. He peeled it up towards him, reached into the narrow gap that it created, and removed the briefcase within. He replaced the floorboard, crawled backwards out of the space and set the oven back to its original spot.

On the kitchen table, he carefully opened the case and surveyed the contents.

'A place for everything, and everything in its place,' he thought.

He reached into a side pocket and removed two passports: one Polish, assigned to 'Gedeon Jaeger', the other Dutch, assigned to one 'Piet Spier'. Both carried the same photo. He slipped them into the inside pocket of his jacket, alongside a neatly folded stack of euros, then closed the briefcase. At the front door, he added a silk cravat, three-quarter length coat, and brown homburg to his already immaculate outward show, and stepped into the sunlight.

He took a long look left and right before setting off

through the slush towards the centre of town. He saw a group of excited schoolchildren making their way to the Cinema Kijow. He saw Gustav, his neighbour and grocer, preparing for the day's trade, and again he saw the crane operators, appearing to make progress with the icicles. In the Main Square, he stopped at the corner of Wislna to watch a chess game outside of a café, lighting a cigarette as the players at the board circled each other mentally, both ignorant of their surroundings as they studied the pieces.

Eventually, Gedeon discreetly threw down his cigarette butt, and watched it simper out, avoiding grinding it into the pavement with the leather moccasins. He strode across the Rynek Glowny towards the Florianska Gate, in the direction of the station. He passed tattoo parlours, bakeries and mini-markets, and then, through the horseshoe form of the Barbican, and finally, the Florianska Gate, that for over half a century had been the passage to the King. He was leaving behind all royal patronage, now.

Beyond the city walls, away from the windbreak of the compacted gothic architecture, the weather was beginning to turn the screw. Gedeon felt it on his nose and even through his leather gloves. He tightened his scarf and raised his coat collar with one hand, keeping a firm grip on the briefcase with the other. An underpass brought him out at the station, and within sight of his train, sitting quietly on the tracks, as if waiting for him alone. He could see it was crowded: women, and wailing children of all ages, pressed up against doors and windows; Silesian-faced men who had known better days, and the generation of commuters that succeeded them; backpackers, railway staff, and fare-dodgers were all crammed in uncomfortably, so tightly that on boarding he could go no further than the doorway. He watched his reflection again, this time in the train window, inches from his face. He looked different now, as he neared his objective.

Most of the passengers would exit at Lobzow, but Gedeon was going furthest. After Lobzow, he took a seat near the train doors that allowed him to stretch the legs that had grown tense from standing. He circled his feet, relishing the fact that he had managed to keep his shoes clean, as the train departed once more. Relaxing further, he removed his hat and gloves and settled them atop the briefcase across his knees. The snow was heavier, with no sign of abating, and Gedeon wondered if the train would be able to complete its journey. The carriage was empty and he could now enjoy the solace, staring out at the white-blanketed fields and occasional tenement housing block. Despite being the only passenger, he kept the case in contact at all times as the train wound its way west. As he mused over the grim, grey, housing projects of Wroclaw that surrounded the station of a city with a dark past, the train doors parted, and a thin old man boarded. He passed Gedeon and sat directly across the aisle from him, facing the rear of the car. Gedeon mused over the man's apparent ignorance, pressing his hands flat on the briefcase, and making a conscious effort to relax. The man wore a starched white collar and a thin black tie. He sat straight-backed in his seat and breathed a few puffs of warmer air into his small hands. The steam circled his head and drew Gedeon's attention to the man's carefully coiffured silver hair, that settled in a firm pompadour over his weathered forehead. The look was completed by a stately white moustache and a pair of round-rimmed spectacles that raised and fell slightly as the man twitched his nose and adapted to the newfound warmth.

They sat in silence as the train coursed through western Poland. As the German border hove into view, the man reached into his left pocket and removed a silver ornamental lighter, the size and shape of a shotgun cartridge. He flicked it open and struck the wheel with his thumb, all in one movement, lighting the cigarette he had placed in his mouth. He threw back his head and took a protracted, enthusiastic drag.

The report of the lighter had turned Gedeon's head, and now he watched the smoke slowly engulf the man's head. He thought of how much he wanted a cigarette himself, but would not ignore the 'no smoking' rule, even when alone in the car. He considered the man arrogant; after all, he himself had abstained. Then, as though pre-empting Gedeon's own disdain, the man spoke.

"Now I am in Germany, I shall do as I damn well please."

He spoke in an English accent that intrigued Gedeon, who was now leaning out of his seat slightly and looking down the aisle through the doors that led to the next carriage, at two guards.

"Excuse me," Gedeon said.

The man unhurriedly finished his cigarette and extinguished it with a skidding motion of his foot, making no attempt to conceal it. It left a sooty smudge on the floor.

The man spoke again. "Still you fear the German authorities, after all these years?"

Gedeon's hands tensed around the corners of the briefcase.

"Light up," the man urged. "I know you're a smoker. I can tell by your fingertips."

Gedeon looked down at his yellowed fingertips without moving his head, then returned his stare to the guards.

"You'll be going to Berlin, are you?" the man enquired.

Gedeon allowed that he was going to "the Prenzlauer Berg area."

"You won't join me?" the man said.

Gedeon furrowed his brow and thought about the offer. He did not want to appear overly keen, but could tell by the man's tone that his presence was requested. The man opened his palm and acknowledged the seat opposite. Gedeon rose and slid across the aisle in a single swift movement, sitting at an angle from the man and leaving a space beside each of them.

"I'm ninety years old," said the man, unprompted, although his age was on Gedeon's mind, "or I will be in three days."

"Then you have seen much," replied Gedeon, looking for an opening.

Noticing the briefcase, the man continued, "I had one just like this, many years ago. They were very useful in my line of work. It's good to know they're still available."

There was an awkward silence.

"How rude of me," said the man, offering his outstretched hand to Gedeon, "Willie Leonard."

Gedeon responded, "Spier."

"A Dutchman?" Willie asked, smiling.

"By birth," lied Gedeon, "but I think myself a Pole. Always."

"But you wear the shoes of a Dutchman, and your briefcase, I believe, is Dutch made. You cannot let go of your roots perhaps, or forget what has gone before. Not so bad, but you are too…" he thought for a moment, "…tense, to be Dutch. Relax. We are alone."

The remark unnerved Gedeon.

"No peace-loving Dutchman would wear a sword-shaped tie-pin though, so maybe you are a Pole. Your name, 'Spier' you say. I trust that's not with two e's…" Willie chuckled inwardly.

His laughter settled Gedeon, who loosened his grip on the briefcase.

Gedeon felt it his turn to interrogate, but less directly.

"What business do you have in Germany?" he asked.

"I'm here at leisure, visiting my daughter, and grandchildren."

Gedeon opened his mouth to speak but Willie had not finished.

"And my great-grandchildren," he added proudly.

Gedeon spoke. "And what does an Englishman of ninety think of Berlin?"

"My thoughts of Berlin are over seventy years old, my friend. I haven't been here since 1936. They are but memories."

Gedeon pondered this. He thought Willie to have been a military man of some capacity, but Berlin, in 1936, almost ten years before the city fell? And now, returning after all this time.

"You are a sportsman, Mr Spier, yes?"

Gedeon gave a slow nod.

"You have a fighter's hands, I suspect a horseman's gait, and a marksman's eyes. A Pentathlete like myself, if ever I saw one."

The information arranged itself in Gedeon's historically-charged brain where it began to make sense. Willie's healthy comportment, a visit to Berlin sixty-five years ago, and the Pentathlon. The Berlin Olympics.

Willie watched an expression of understanding and curiosity play on Gedeon's face.

"I did *not* salute," said Willie defiantly. He folded his arms as he spoke and curled his bottom lip up.

"The Olympics," said Gedeon. "You took part?"

"I had no intention of going really," Willie explained,

"jumping through hoops, almost literally on that bloody horse, for those Nazi bastards. The so-called Modern Pentathlon. So 'modern' that they wouldn't allow the Jews to enter."

Gedeon smiled.

"I was full of it back then, of course. The folly of youth and all. I went from shelling Franco from a hole in the Spanish dirt, to prancing around on horseback in front of Hitler, in the space of a few days." Willie thought back for a second, then added, "It was us who were getting shelled, most of the time. At Huesca. Me and a fella, name of Eric, fancied himself a writer, he did. Got shot in the neck, survived, but... anyway, I took him back to Barcelona for treatment. I looked around the injury ward and decided I could be put to better use elsewhere."

Gedeon interrupted, "So, you went to the Games?"

"I was supposed to travel with the team but as I'd no intention of competing, I buggered off to Spain a few months before the Games. After the hospital visit, I was walking along the Ramblas and saw a young Spaniard tinkering with an old motorbike and sidecar. The three of them looked like they'd seen better days, especially the sidecar. I say 'tinkering', he was more like smashing it up with a hammer for parts. It looked like a Triumph at first glance, probably brought over by the International Brigade boys from back home. I knew them well as my father had been a dispatch rider, and he was always messing around with bikes. Anyway, this fella was cursing it upside down in Catalan, I think. I couldn't understand a word but it was obvious he'd had enough of it."

"You bought it?" Gedeon asked.

"Not quite. All I had with me was a rusty old misfiring Mauser pistol, and a box of cigars. The gun was non-negotiable, especially in the middle of Barcelona during a civil war, although the safest place to be when it was fired was in front of it. I used to just wave it around a bit to get people out of my way. I gave him the cigars and offered to take the bike, on the condition that it started first go. It did, and made a noise like the crack of doom. Half an hour later, I left the barracks with everything I owned, which wasn't much at all. I rode night and day, through France, and Germany. The sidecar and I separated somewhere near St. Etienne, which was a blessing in disguise as I didn't need it. I swerved to avoid some cyclists and the car struck a tree and broke clean away from the bike. I went off one side of the road and the sidecar the other. I lay in the mud thinking about whether the Spaniard had gotten the best part of the deal with those cigars, and by then it looked like he probably had."

Willie stopped talking and lit another cigarette. Gedeon was emboldened enough by Willie's adventurous exploits to spark up a cigarette of his own. He used Willie's lighter and ignored the presence of the guards. He inhaled and sat back as Willie continued.

"I spent two days in the barn of a French farmer, fixing up the bike. His English was as bad as my French but we muddled through and I made it to Berlin soon after.

It wasn't ideal preparation for the Olympics, though. You could have lifted me off the bike and straight onto my horse and I wouldn't have known the difference."

"That's a good story," said Gedeon, "but does it have a happy…"

Willie interjected, "I won silver."

"Oh. That's very good. But you were second best."

Willie looked at his cigarette for longer than was comfortable.

"I had other things on my mind," said Willie.

"Of course. The journey. The accident," said Gedeon.

"Yes. But there were other things… I was approached."

"Approached?" said Gedeon.

"The riding and the fencing went well but the night before, I was invited to a reception with some of the various nations' Olympic committee members. I shouldn't have gone, the night before competition and all, but I was never one to turn down a party. The Swedish women's swimming team was going to be there."

Willie's eyes twinkled, and a smile stretched across his lips.

"So there I was, dancing away, with this Swedish girl, Elin, having a good time of it; the Games were the last thing on my mind, while the top brass sat around us, twitching their moustaches. Later on, Elin and I were suitably acquainted, and I was ready for a nightcap and a private swimming lesson, if you know what I mean."

"Yes, yes," said Gedeon, smiling.

Willie finished his cigarette and again crushed it into

the floor. Gedeon did the same but not before he had sub-consciously looked around for an ashtray.

"Behind the tables, I'd noticed a couple of the old boys watching us, and now they had their heads together, talking discreetly. As Elin was pulling on her coat, one of the waiters handed me a note from the two men. I remember thinking that if the content of the note didn't result in me waking up next to a member of the Swedish women's swimming team, then I wasn't interested. They wanted me to visit their hotel room upstairs, for a chat. My curiosity got the better of me so I sent Elin on to her room and told her I'd join her soon enough. Their room was on the eighth floor and they took an age to answer the door, which aroused my suspicions immediately. Inside there was a third man, who to my knowledge hadn't been at the reception. I was introduced to each in turn, and offered a drink, which I declined. The third man did most of the talking. In a very relaxed manner, he briefed me, in excellent English, on recent political events, before moving on to European history, and finishing with a stern lecture on the evils of Fascism, which included nothing I didn't already know."

As the train entered Berlin, Gedeon noticed the two guards talking animatedly to each other as they pointed out of the window, and wondered if there might be a delay.

Willie started up again, "Then they told me something I didn't know."

"What was that?" Gedeon asked.

"They said that Hitler was attending the competition the next morning in Wannsee. They wanted me to…"

Gedeon interrupted, making a gun gesture with his thumb and forefinger, jokingly at first, but then his mind turned serious.

"He was coming to watch Franck Langsam, the great German medal hope at the time. The plan was for me to get a shot away as Langsam took his. That way, all of the spectators, and especially the High Command, would all be watching him. The logistics of the whole thing were complicated. I'd have needed a clear shot without making it obvious that I was aiming at ol' Adolf, that is, without stretching my arm, as such. Then I needed to escape from Germany. Impossible. I could have saved a lot of people a lot of trouble if I'd gone through with it."

"You'd be the man who prevented the biggest war in history," said Gedeon.

"But we wouldn't have known that then, of course," Willie said.

Both men reflected on the past, then Gedeon thought of the future. He was taking a similar course to Willie's all those years before, but quite possibly wouldn't have had to if Willie had been persuaded by the three men in the hotel room.

The train moved through Berlin as the two new acquaintances sat in reflective silence. Gedeon felt a mild pang of guilt for not being wholly honest about who he was, and soon the lie would grow as he now intended to get off at a different stop to his intended one as a cover of sorts.

"A man with the courage of his convictions can change the course of history," said Gedeon.

"Or avenge it," said Willie, as he rose from his seat.

The train squealed to a sudden stop. Gedeon was impressed that a man of Willie's age had no need to support himself against the handrail. Willie cast a final glance at the guards, adjusted his glasses, and stepped out onto Gedeon's original stop at Friedrichstrasse. Gedeon stayed calm and did a quick mental inventory of Berlin's train network, at the same time wondering how he was going to get back to Friedriechstrasse to make his appointment.

He quickly visited the station washroom as he rescheduled in his head. The graffiti-ridden wall tiles, barely visible in the poor light, were cracked and chipped. An icy breeze hissed through the vents as he checked himself in the mirror on the way out. In the low lighting, his reflection was almost a silhouette, as far removed from his image that morning as it was possible to be. Moving closer to the mirror, he saw his face in the half light. The right side was angelic, ethereal; the left though, was flooded with darkness. The black shadows had filled his eye socket, his sallow cheek bones and the freshly opened pores as he splashed water onto his skin, but the eyes themselves were no longer the crystal marbles of the morning. Now they were dark with intent and furious purpose, and through them he saw the man he had to be.

'Or avenge it.' Willie's parting words came to mind.

He took a single deep breath, then stifled a cough, before turning towards the doorway. A taxi appeared and Gedeon's right arm instinctively shot out to hail it. The car swerved sharply towards the kerbside, splashing heavy grey slush over the path. Sensing the threat, he shuffled back, curling his toes up with a satisfied smile. He dropped into the rear of the car and proffered a twenty euro note over the driver's shoulder.

"Friedrichstrasse," said Gedeon, firmly, in heavily-accented Dutch.

"Ja," replied the driver.

"Raus," added Gedeon.

He made a point of avoiding eye contact in the rear view mirror, and lowered the brim of his hat as a precaution.

The driver was startled by Gedeon's offering for the short distance, but sensed enough not to ask questions. He knew he needed to avoid the heavy traffic of the main routes and take the quickest route possible. Gedeon needed to move swiftly, directly and unnoticed since crossing the border, and now he could. He quietly referenced the driver's identity card hanging from the mirror and admired the car's immaculate interior: clean, sterile, functional and defined. As they moved purposefully through the Oranienburger district, Gedeon noticed how the locals moved in a more organised fashion than their Polish counterparts when a group of schoolchildren crossed the road ahead. They walked almost in step, contrary to the disorganised group he had seen that morning at the cinema in Krakow.

The car left Linienstrasse, joining Friedrichstrasse at its northern junction with Oranienburgerstrasse. The driver threw the car left and sped south towards Kreuzeberg, and the infamous Checkpoint Charlie, a relic of an oppressive regime that still rankled with Gedeon.

The driver stared directly ahead as Gedeon departed smoothly at Freiderichstrasse, disappearing amongst the commuters. He descended to the car park beneath the station and carefully approached a specifically a silver Porsche 997.

Gedeon reached beneath the driver's side rear wheel arch of the Porsche and carefully ran his left hand across the tyre surface until he felt the key, and scraped it into his palm. He quickly scanned the carpark, turned his body towards the rusty white Fiat Uno parked in the next space, and slid the key into the driver's door. With a flick of his wrist, the slush-stained white door unlocked and he swung the briefcase beneath the driver's seat and lowered himself onto the coarse, brown upholstery. He adjusted the seat, steering column and mirrors, and the air-conditioning dial, which was set to 'cold,' and fired the ignition. The engine sparked and he sidled away unnoticed amid the reassuring rattle and rumble of the 1 litre engine.

The brown bricked houses of Hoorn loomed nosily over the cobbled streets below as the canal sneaked unnoticed between them before escaping into the vastness of the

Ijsselmeer. The winter sun strafed the harbour and the fishing boats that bobbed contentedly on the water's surface. Hungry kingfishers skimmed across the horizon, soaring, then plummeting like stones at the glimpse of a potential bite. The town centre markets were doing their usual healthy trade, mainly in cheese: wheels of cheddar stacked like tyres alongside wedges of Gouda, the familiar red balls of Edam, Emmental, and Old Amsterdam. Abel thought the locals looked like ants, crawling among the stalls, as he looked down on them from his apartment over the Grote Noord. His view was restricted by the blind that was almost always lowered, as he stood back from the window, not wanting to be seen.

Sunlight squeezed through the thin gap between blind and window, but revealed nothing of Abel's living arrangements. He plodded backwards across the thin carpet and rested his body into the armchair that fitted him like a well-worn coat. It knew the contours of his slouching back, the roll of his shoulders, and the angle of his head, always cocked away from the window. With his bony hands, he carefully packed his pipe with potent South American tobacco. The sharp smell reminded Abel of times in warmer climes. The hems of his trousers rode up to the tops of his grey socks as he reclined in his chair, contemplating his imminent grocery trip. He secured the pipe between his lips and slowly swung his legs back onto the carpet, heaving his spindly upper body out of its niche.

Releasing a wheezy breath into the dry air, he reached

for his coat and hat. Despite his infirmity, he shunned the convenience of the lift, and took the stairs to the building's lobby, where he took a deep breath of warm air and let himself out onto the edge of the marketplace. He stooped as he walked through Rode Steen and could have saved time crossing the square, through the eyeline of Hoorn's most famous son, the bloodthirsty sailor Jan Pieterszoon Coen, whose statue looks out to far off lands, but Abel preferred the psychological security of the wall line.

Gedeon flicked on the Fiat's headlights, illuminating the signs for Osnabruck, as the daylight began to fade. He stopped on the outskirts of the city at a deserted industrial estate of storage containers and abandoned machinery. For a few seconds, he relished the silence. The journey had done nothing to dull his senses, which grew sharper with the coming nightfall. He stepped from the car and walked to the rear, removing a pocket knife from his jacket. It was the first time the briefcase had been out of his sight since he left the house that morning. Using the knife as a screwdriver, he detached the car's number plates. He then opened the car boot and removed two new plates and a large metal paint tin. From his trouser pocket, he took his lighter, train ticket stub and a handful of toilet paper he had taken from the washroom and placed them on the ground. He turned his attention back to the car, attaching the new Dutch marked plates, and pocketing the knife.

He then broke the original plates in half, muffling the cracking sound with the hem of his coat, and threw them into the paint tin with the paper, which he then set his lighter to until the flames took hold. It would be several more hours before he reached his destination and now, under cover of early evening, he felt comfortable enough to remove his coat. He folded it over his arm and placed it in the passenger seat footwell in front of the briefcase.

The car disappeared amongst the warehouses briefly, and reappeared on the slip road that eventually returned Gedeon to the Autobahn.

The weight of the shopping pulled Abel's body down even lower as he returned home. By the time he reached his front door, the market crowds had dispersed under threat of rain. He was relieved to set the bags down on the doorstep as he searched for his key, but knew he would have to lift them twice more before he was finished. Inside the flat, he locked the door, in the comforting knowledge that he would not have to leave for another week, or longer. He was too exhausted from the walk to put the groceries away, or even take them to the kitchen, and instead left them beside the door and collapsed back into his seat, still in his hat and coat, where he slumped until early the following morning.

Gedeon considered the sound geometry of the Dutch countryside as the car cut across the flat plains of Hilversum. A man of simple pleasures, he appreciated the minimalism of the scenery, punctuated by the occasional windmill, or farmhouse, and the assuring straightness of the waterways. Everything seemed so neat, symmetrical, even in the dark. He turned north out of Hilversum and headed in to the Hook of Holland.

Abel's long sleep had left him still more tired when he awoke. He slowly remembered the task of putting away yesterday's shopping. His mind was alert but his body was sluggish and he struggled to climb out of the chair. He stretched lightly before bending down towards the bags and lifting them once more, heaving them onto the kitchen table and starting to empty them. He reached the jar of Brazilian coffee at the bottom of one of the bags and broke off from his duty to prepare a drink. He was meticulous in his preparation, adding the coffee last to avoid scorching them with the hot water. It was a thick blend that finally found its way to Abel's dry lips, as he secured the cup between both hands. The vapours curled around the cup and then out across the apartment, finding their way under the door and into the hall. Even the handyman detected a faint hint of what he thought was Arabica as he ascended the staircase in the hall. On hearing his knock, Abel did his usual trick of feigning ignorance, but the handyman was persistent. He became impatient, and eventually called out, "Verwarming controleren."

Abel's Dutch was not so good, by choice. He rarely spoke to anybody, but understood the basics of the language. He also knew that it was cold enough for the apartment committee to have arranged for heating checks at that time of year.

"Een half uur," the janitor shouted.

Abel took another pull on the coffee cup and closed his eyes. 'Half an hour' he could live with, if it meant a reliable heating system to see him through the remaining winter.

He settled the coffee cup on the table and hobbled towards the door. Through the spyhole, he saw a man in red overalls holding a battered brown tool bag and wearing a frayed, blue, baseball cap.

The man's impatience peaked as Abel opened the various locks. At the last one, he paused, then spoke confidently, even with his aged rasping voice.

"Identificatie," he said.

The man reached into his pocket and produced a laminated card that he held up to the spyhole. Abel squinted as he checked the details. The man was from an Amsterdam-based home repairs company. Abel opened the final lock and put on the safety chain. He inspected the man through the gap in the door. The man said nothing, instead raising his bag slightly, to acknowledge the tools. Abel unhooked the chain and drew the door towards him, the gap barely wide enough for the man to enter.

The man looked at Abel, who was still wearing his topcoat and hat.

"Koud, huh?" he said, affecting a shivering motion.

Abel nodded.

The man threw the bag beneath the window and studied the radiator on the wall beside it. He reached to open the blind, to create more light, as Abel winced and retreated into the kitchen area. The man reached inside the bag and began to adjust some of his tools. Abel heard a series of metallic clicks and screwing squeaks as he stared into the black maelstrom of his coffee, the fumes flushing his eyes. The man peered over the window ledge at the Groot Noord marketplace, and saw a white Fiat Uno pull slowly away from the kerb at the junction of West Kerk, then returned to his tools.

"Uitzetten," he said, making a circular turning motion with his right hand.

Abel stepped into the passageway and padded slowly towards the thermostat.

The man closed the blind, removed his overalls and cap, and stuffed them into the bag. Then he calmly sat down on the chair in the corner of the room, facing the doorway at a slight angle.

Abel was unphased by the man's sudden transformation, or that he was resting a gun calmly on his thigh with his right hand. Gedeon thrust it at Abel's chair in the centre of the room. Abel settled into it, but bolt upright, this time.

"My only regret is that I have lived this long," he said.

Gedeon remained silent. He had not expected resistance but was thrown slightly by Abel's candour.

He knew not to let his guard down. Whatever Abel's condition, Gedeon allowed no sympathy.

"I can tell by your shoes that you are not who you say you are. From the heating place. No, never," said Abel, smiling. "And I know that your people will find my people, at any cost, so I let you in. Otherwise, you get in some other way."

Abel reached for his pipe and commenced where he had left off before he'd gone shopping. He contemplated Gedeon's gun.

"A Taurus Millennium," he said. "A good model. PT145 I would guess. Silencer is handmade, no?"

Gedeon nodded, silently impressed with Abel's knowledge.

"From Porto Allegre," said Abel. "As you know, I spent time in Brazil. I carried something similar. It is sometimes wild there."

"For protection..." said Gedeon, "...from discovery?"

Abel sucked on his pipe and considered Gedeon's accent. "You are a Pole. Aniol smierci," he said.

'Aniol smierci,' thought Gedeon. *'The Death Angel.'* He liked the tag but did not show it.

"Ya, for protection, of course. Lots of gangs, you understand? Certain races are, how I put this, more..." he waved his pipe, then tailed off.

Gedeon looked right through him then reached into his inside pocket and removed a padded white envelope that he tossed into Abel's lap. Abel continued to smoke his pipe, ignoring the envelope.

"My life's work," Abel said, "the extermination of fifteen thousand Jews, reduced to a sheet of paper."

Gedeon bristled. His eyes widened as he gripped the gun tighter.

Abel was as relaxed and lucid as he had ever been.

"Do you think you are the first Jew that has wanted, or even tried, to kill me?" he asked.

"No. But I will be the last," Gedeon answered.

"That I am certain of," Abel continued. "A hero amongst your people. The man who caught Abelard Hahn. What is my price? Am I the last? No, no, no. Of course not. What of Djemanjuk? And Heim? You put them in court, to show how civilised you can be, yet here you are, executing old men in peaceful towns where nobody is any the wiser." He stopped for a reaction. Nothing. "You are as bloodthirsty as the men you condemn, but, credit to you, you get the job done. Quietly." He acknowledged the gun's silencer once again. "You are a craftsman, I see. A nice job. Not something I have seen before. Not on a Taurus. Can cause quite a… a… what is the word? A 'commotion' with a piece like that."

Gedeon interjected, "Your friend Djemanjuk is being dealt with by the Americans. In Europe, he would suffer the same fate as you. A spinning bullet, Brazilian made, of course, straight through his skull."

Abel cut in, "But Heim has eluded you for so long."

"Heim is dead," said Gedeon, calmly.

"That story makes good reading for your people, and justifies many thousands of your wasted shekels,' said Abel, chuckling to himself, 'but I must ask you, where was this determination seventy years ago?"

Gedeon's eyes swelled with fury.

"Now you hide in the shadows, stalking your target, then strike when they are weakest. A frail old man like me," Abel said, his eyes closing slowly.

Gedeon looked around the room, taking his eyes off his prey for a moment, and studied the austere straight lines of the modest apartment, framed by rows of bookshelves. The editions they supported looked dated, covering a wide range of subjects. Most appeared to be in English: ancient history, engineering, and theology, mainly, and the occasional classic. Gedeon spotted faded versions of Conrad's *Heart Of Darkness*, and *Lord Of The Flies*. Stories of survival, he noted. Behind them, sterile white wallpaper deflecting what little daylight was allowed in. It lit the whites of Abel's watery blue eyes when he opened them, as slowly as he had closed them a moment earlier.

"You admire my collection?" he said.

"You are a man of words?" said Gedeon.

"I am a man of deeds," said Abel. "As are you."

"We are not alike," said Gedeon, firmly.

"But, of course we are. The blue eyes. The methodical way of doing things. Which is a very German trait, I must say. We have much in common. An admiration of literature, perhaps."

Gedeon shifted in his seat slightly as Abel scanned the shelves.

"At the camp I would have the 'kinder,' the children, you understand, read to me. They could hardly hold the books for trembling, those poor Juden. My favourite was always *Der Kleine Prinz*."

Gedeon's eyes fell across the book spines until they reached *Le Petit Prince*, Saint-Exupery's enduring fable.

"This book has many solutions for life's difficulties," Abel said, sitting up in his chair.

"Now the Nazi will read for the Jew," ordered Gedeon, motioning with his gun at the shelf.

Abel approached the shelf and reached for the book, bound in blue suede, and very carefully removed it from its slot. Gedeon noticed the dust on and around the area of the book's space. It had not been moved for some time.

"You do not work alone, do you?" asked Abel. "You have a support team, yes, to cover your tracks. Cleaners?"

Gedeon maintained his silence.

Making himself comfortable once more, Abel rested the book on his lap, angling it slightly upwards.

He swept his hand across the cover, throwing the dust into the tense atmosphere, and opened it, seemingly at random. His left hand hovered over the page as he stifled a dust-induced coughing fit with his right. The coughing was just loud enough to stifle the sound of him pulling back the slide of the Sauer P230 concealed inside the book and setting it to a single-action position. He steadied the book with his right hand and again appeared to sweep the page off with his left, but instead squeezed the Sauer's cold steel trigger. The round blew apart the tops of the pages and shattered the book's suede veneer as it escaped the cloud of smoke and prose and corkscrewed across the room.

The remains of the book thudded into Abel's bony groin, before settling against his stomach. The bullet bored through Gedeon's right cheek bone and caromed around the lower half of his face, dragging with it sinew, air and tissue, before exiting impatiently below his right ear. It was a messy departure, that saw most of the aftermath spilling onto Gedeon's overalls. The gluey detritus thudded onto the carpet and became entwined in the fibres.

Gedeon's head hung to the right, as if willingly pouring the contents out onto the floor, as the *blup... blup... blup* sound of them hitting the carpet beat through the room. The small amount of smoke cleared, but Abelard could not see. His eyes were closed again, as he lay back in his chair, waiting for the cleaners to arrive.

THE TUNLEY HUM

"It's out there, Brenda. Somewhere. I'm telling ya. I don't know where, or what, or how. But it's out there."

A wisp of steam from Ron's cup of tea began to melt the condensation from the bedroom window.

"Don't be so bloody daft, Ron," Brenda said. "Drink your tea."

"I can hear it. Or feel it. Or bloody summat," Ron continued.

"You wanna' get to the friggin' doctors, I think," Brenda suggested, giving a short shrift that comes naturally over forty years of marriage.

"For him to tell me it's bloody tinnitus, again?" He turned from the window, with a thoughtful look on his face.

"It might be tinnitus," Brenda said. "All that bloody racket down the steelworks."

"I'm two bloody years retired, Brenda," Ron said, losing his patience, "and this only started about six months ago. And what about Keith?"

"What about Keith?" Brenda asked.

"I worked right bloody next to him for twenty-two years and there's nothing wrong with his ears."

"His ears are about the only thing that *do* work," she

replied. "His bloody eyesight's not up to much. He can't see where Pablo's shitting when he's walking him, for a start. Frigging mess out there on that front with that bloody dog."

"Never mind the dog," Ron said, "someone needs to find out what's going on, with this… with this bloody… whatever it is."

Men, and it's almost always men, become embroiled in all kinds of pointless distractions once they retire, and sometimes before. The distractions are exactly that, distractions, and rarely productive. I once knew a man who spent his days inspecting manhole covers for damage and signs of disrepair and at the end of each week reported them to a bemused local authority. He was performing a service of sorts, but I often felt he could have put his time to better use. Presumably, there was point in his life when it suddenly occurred to him that the moment he was free from the shackles of gainful employment, he could realise his real vocation of inspecting manhole covers.

When I asked him about it, he said, "Well, if I don't do it, nobody else will," as though he'd imbued the issue with a great importance, another thing men of a certain age always seem to do, in order to create a sense of purpose. Anyway, he's dead now. Yep. You guessed it.

Around six months ago, Ron Airely had noticed a persistent humming, somewhere. He couldn't pinpoint where. He could *just* hear it, or feel it. He was out walking the fields that stretched across Tunley Moor. There was the noticeable hum of the pylons, but this was something else, far from any pylon. It stayed with him, not the memory of it, but the hum itself. It followed him home, and into the house. It slept with him. It watched the television with him. It came down the phone line, and up through the plumbing. It wouldn't go away.

"I'm going to the Herald about it," he announced one day, referring to the local paper.

"I wouldn't," Brenda said. "They'll make you do one of them daft pictures of you looking glum and pointing at a pylon or something, like they did with them daft buggers who couldn't get a meat pie."

He was sitting at his computer, vainly researching, when his grandson entered.

"Dylan," he said, "have you ever heard anything like a bloody hum, just, like, in the air, or something?"

Dylan didn't respond.

"Dylan," Brenda said, "your Grandad's talking to you."

"Me?" Dylan replied, pointing at himself. He removed an earbud that was connected to his mobile phone.

"Look at this," Ron said, pointing at the computer, "you ever heard of these things, where there's just a humming noise all the time?"

"Be 5G or summat," Dylan said, reinserting his earbuds.

"Dylan, take them bloody things out of your ears," Brenda scolded.

"To do with mobile phones n' tha," Dylan added.

"Well, you're always wired up to some bloody thing or other," Ron said. "What's it all about? Can't you hear that?"

"Hear what?"

"It says 'ere," Ron continued, looking back at his computer screen, "an invasive, continuous droning."

"Continuous droning?" Brenda said. "Yes, I think I'm experiencing it now."

Dylan grinned then said, "There was this radio station, once, like, in the olden days, like 1980s or whatever, in, I think it was in America, and the signal was like super powerful. It was like, the signal was like getting conducted through metal so it was in the cutlery, in people's houses, and coming through the pots and pans."

He laughed aloud at the thought it.

"Does your mother know you're on drugs, son?" Ron interrupted dryly.

"Ron!" Brenda shouted.

"A friggin' radio signal coming through the soddin' egg whisk? I ask yer!"

"It was even broadcasting through people's mattresses, like, what used to be inside mattresses, Grandma?"

"They used to have like coiled springs in 'em," Brenda added, "years ago."

"Yeah, like that," Dylan said.

"A radio station coming through your mattress..." Brenda mused. "What'll they think of next?"

"I'll google it," Dylan offered, scrolling through his phone. "Ere, look" he said, proffering the phone.

Ron adjusted his glasses.

"W... L... W in the 1930s...the 1930s, Dylan! Not the bloody 1980s! Your mother would have had Adam bloody Ant pulsing through her duvet if it was in the 1980s."

"Oooh, your mam loved Adam Ant, Dylan."

"I... I... don't know what that is?" Dylan said, looking puzzled.

"It was in America," Ron continued. "Five hundred kilowatts, blasting out to half the world, it says 'ere. So, just goes to show, doesn't it?"

"Show what?" Brenda said.

"That, y'know, I'm not going bloody mad."

"Radio Tunley, can I help?"

"Yes, I bloody well hope so," Ron replied, holding his mobile phone in the hands free position. "What's your frequency?"

"Excuse me, sir?"

"The frequency of the station. Your outtage, or whatever."

"Well, I, er... er..."

"Is it over five hundred and fifty watts?"

The line went dead.

"Christ on a bloody bike," Ron said, to no one in particular, growing exasperated. "They're chasing me around with a constant humming but they can't even connect you on the telephone."

"Hello, is that the news desk?" Ron asked, beginning his next line of enquiry with the local paper.

"Yes, the Herald."

"Right, I've got a story for you. I'm sure you've had lots of similar reports. It's about this humming."

"What humming? I'll need some details first."

"Well, I'm bloody well gonna give you 'em, now," Ron said.

"Name, please."

"Ron."

"Surname, Ron?"

"Yes, I've got one, thanks, now about this humming…"

"I'll need to take more details. Address, Ron?"

"This is the Turley Herald, is it not?" Ron questioned. "Or have I bloody well rang up the National Security Agency by mistake?"

"It is the Turley Herald, yes."

"Righto… I want to know what's going on with this humming, that's… going around."

"I'm not aware of it. What does it sound like?"

"It's like, well, it's like a… a hum. Like a humming sound. Constant."

"Loud? Quiet?"

"Er, well it's just there."

"And where's it coming from, this 'hum'?"

"Bloody hellfire, son. Who's the journalist here, me or you?"

"We don't really investigate instances of people hearing things. Not enough substance to it, really, unless you're willing to have your picture taken, next to a pylon, say."

"Is that right?" Ron said, bubbling with indignation.

"Well?" said the voice at the other end.

"Not enough substance?" Ron said, loudly. "Last week you did a piece about a pigeon flying around the friggin' town hall."

"Animal stories always go over well, Ron."

"Well, let's pretend then, that this humming, is from… a… a…" he grasped for an idea.

"A hummingbird?" came the voice.

"Don't be clever with me, son. I used to use that so-called newspaper for shinpads before you were even thought of," Ron cracked. "So, you're not interested?"

"Er, frankly no, sorry. Have you tried your local authority?"

"You mean the council? Them buggers couldn't organise a fart in a curry house."

"Tunley Council, can I help?"

"I'm not sure I'm through to the right place, here, to do with… er… noise pollution stuff," Ron explained.

"Yes. This is the right department."

"Well, what it is, is…"

"I'll need some details first."

"Righto. Name, address, all that?"

"Yes, please."

"The name's Ron, but can I just sound you out on the thing first, then?"

"Yeah. Of course you can, Ron, go for it."

"There's a humming and I've noticed it over the past few months, and I don't know where it's coming from but it's constant."

"This may sound like a bit of a joke question, Ron, but it's not tinnitus, is it?"

"No, love, it's not tinnitus. What I want to know is, is there any sort of development or radiographic, or whatever the word is, work, going on that might have caused it."

"I'm not aware of anything, Ron, but I can certainly ask our environmental team to take a look at it, or rather, have a listen."

"Can you do that? It's driving me bloody mad."

"Whereabouts do you think it might be coming from, Ron?"

"Well, I first noti… are you still there?"

The line broke off, then reconnected.

The operator said, "Ron, are you still there?"

"Yeah. Can you hear me?"

"Yeah, you're back, now."

"I dunno what happened there. Anyway, I was walking over Tunley Moor a few months ago…"

"Near the pylons?" the operator asked.

"Yeah, near the pylons, but it's not the pylons. I know what the pylons sound like. They sort of crackle. It's not that."

"Okay."

"And I've heard it ever since. At night. In bed. I'm

thinking could it be something to do with a farm. Some animal deterrent, maybe?"

"Possibly, Ron, but it sounds very, er, invasive, if you like, especially if you can hear it in the house."

"It bloody is."

"Have any of your neighbours noticed it?"

"Not one of them, not that we bother with them much. I mean I haven't been knocking door-to-door, y'know, but I haven't heard anything."

"Except the hum," the operator joked.

"Yeah," Ron laughed, "except the hum." He felt he was making progress. Someone was listening.

"What did the council say?" Brenda asked, later that day.

"They're gonna have a look at it. Or a listen at it."

"I bet you can't hear it tomorrow, anyway," she said.

"Why not?" Ron asked.

"The joiners are coming to do them kitchen tops. They'll be cutting and banging all bloody day."

"There's dogshit all over out there, love," said Barry, as he lugged his equipment from the van, into the hallway the next morning.

"I know, it's that bloody dog of Keith's," Brenda said, welcoming the workmen for the day.

"There's another lad. Terry. In the van. He'll be through shortly," Barry said.

"My husband's gone walking over the Moor so he won't be stood over you all day."

"That's how we like it, love," Barry said, placing down his tools, and waving Terry from the van.

"I'll leave you to it, then," Brenda said, wandering into the living room.

"Watch out for that shit, Tekka. Don't wanna be traipsing that in and out," Barry shouted from the hallway, as Terry stepped from the van.

"What's that?" Terry asked, looking skyward.

"The shit. The dogshite, there," shouted Barry, pointing.

"I mean the noise," Terry replied.

"What noise?" Barry said.

"You can't hear that?" Terry said, rhetorically.

"Howay, man."

"It's like a dentist's fucking drill," Terry shouted.

"Well, you'd know with them fucking teeth. Howay."

Barry approached the house, and Brenda, who had returned to the doorway on overhearing.

"How do you put up with that?" Terry asked, waving his free hand around his ear.

She gave a long shake of the head. "You, and my husband, are the only people who can hear that, whatever it is. He'll be over the bloody moon when he finds out someone else can hear it. How would you describe it?"

"Just like… a… sort of deep droning," Terry explained.

"He's been onto the council, the paper, everyone," she said.

At that, Barry fired up a bandsaw in the kitchen that was loud enough to startle Brenda.

"That'll drown it out, I bet," she smiled.

"I can still hear it," Terry said, grimacing.

Shortly afterwards, Ron returned from his morning stroll over the Moor.

"I can't take any more of that," he said, explaining his early return to Brenda as he stepped into the house. "I'd rather listen to this all day." He gestured into the kitchen where the work was taking place.

"I can hear that, mate," Terry said, looking up from his work, wincing.

"Well, bloody hell. I ask yer. I'm going bloody mad, here, son and she's telling me it's all in my head," Ron said, somewhat relieved.

"Noticed it as soon as I got out of the van, mate. It's giving me a headache to be honest," Terry said. He rubbed his temples.

"You wanna lay off the fucking gear on a weekend, you, mate," Barry cracked, quietly so neither Brenda nor Ron could hear.

"The council are supposed to be investigating," Ron said. "It's just there, all the time. Do you live round about, son?"

"I'm from over Chesney way, mate. Never heard 'owt like it over there or anything."

"Right," Ron said, prompting Brenda into action, "write this down, that he's from Chesney, which is what, about fifteen miles away?"

"About that," Barry interrupted, inspecting off-cuts of wood, "next town over from Cloud Cuckooland."

He and Brenda smirked at the remark, as Terry let out a long groan and lowered himself to the kitchen floor, resting his head and back against one of the cupboards.

"I think you lads better have five minutes," Brenda said. "I'll put kettle on."

"They've just bloody got here, haven't they?" Ron asked, looking at his watch.

Terry rubbed his temples again, and this time his ears. As he reached for his mobile phone, he noticed tiny red specks dotted across the palm of his hand. He touched his ear again. More specks, this time more vivid. Sharper. A stronger red. Almost black. He blew sawdust from his index finger and inserted it into his right ear. He drew it out to see that it was covered with blood all the way down to its first joint.

"Fuck," he said, staring at the finger, as Barry moved to inspect it.

"You're bloody bleeding, son. Your ears. Bloody hell, Bren, look at the lad," Ron said, looking shocked.

"You are n'all," Barry said. "You wanna get that looked at."

"You better go to the hospital, son," Brenda said, fiddling with cotton wool balls from the kitchen draw.

"It's the humming what's got 'im, I'm telling yer," Ron said, almost satisfactorily.

It was everyone's natural inclination to check their own ears. Brenda's mouth fell open as she looked in the hallway mirror to see thin streams of blood running down the side of her face.

"Roonnn... Ronnnnnn..." she said, panicking, looking from her hands to her reflection, as if caught between the two.

Ron didn't react. Couldn't react. He stood frozen in the kitchen doorway, as blood streamed from both ears and pooled in the sawdust from the carpentry. He suddenly clutched at his chest and, almost doubled up, fell to the floor.

Terry was unconscious now, slumped against the cupboard door with his chin on his chest.

Waves of nausea swept over Brenda, beginning to slowly paralyse her. She took a short gulp of air and plunged head first into the hallway mirror. It slid down the wall then tipped away when it hit the skirting board, bouncing and coming to rest over her curled up body, her knees tucked into her chest.

Barry lurched forward, off balance, falling against the dormant bandsaw, smashing his chest against the worktop on his way to the floor.

In the still open doorway of the house shuddered the postman, kneeling over his sack, death-rattling in a pool of blood.

At the garden gate, Keith, who had come for his customary nose into whatever home improvements were going on, lay supine on the pavement, still holding the dog lead as Pablo sniffed at his blood-stained ear.

Like most men and their obsessions, Ron Airey never was able to establish the source of what became known as

The Tunley Hum, that had followed him from the Moor that day, and so greatly occupied him for that strange six or so months, and would go on to eliminate almost a third of the world's population.

COME TO KEPLER

"I think we're definitely lost, now," I say for something like the fourth time since we left the Spaceport fifteen minutes ago.

I've been lost in all corners of the Earth, but never in Outer Space, or out of Inner Space, or wherever we are now. I know we're on Kepler 22b, which is our holiday destination, but beyond that, I have no real bearings. Karen's reading the brochure, trying not to appear pissed off, even though she is... *I've* apparently gotten us lost. I'm quietly raging, my default setting, because there hasn't been a single point of reference for almost 150km, which, to add to the confusion, are Kepler Miles, and not kilometres. Only an urban planning department staffed by Earthlings could come up with something so stupid. I'm driving something called a Dust Bus. It's essentially an SUV, but it hovers, and goes underwater.

No one other than the manufacturer knows how, or even why, it would need to do this. I haven't seen a drop of natural water anywhere.

It had taken me half an hour to start it because the thumbprint recognition technology at the pick-up point wasn't working properly.

"Are you using your own thumb?" asked the infuriatingly calm robot that was taking care of the 'handover'... or 'thumbover'.

No. I have a pocketful of dismembered thumbs I collected when I was a despotic Vietcong Army Colonel back in the 1960s.

"Thumb not recognised," it parroted.

How about I stick it up your arse and see if it registers that way?

The robot called me 'sir' proving that nowhere in the Solar System could you escape the elitism of Earth.

"It's a 'she'," Karen whispered, after I continuously referred to the robot as 'it'. She gave a disapproving look between me and the robot, which was wearing a name badge, Maria. She/It was conceived by an American company called Karels, one the many US private contractors that have carved up the planet between them.

Maria has a vaguely Hispanic accent.

"You mean 'she's' a 'she'?" I'd added.

Maria was trying to do everything for us. It was dehumanising. If you're happy to lie on your settee all day, and shout into a plastic canister when you want to listen to a particular song, or order a week's worth of shopping that, on arrival, contains nothing you actually asked for, then Kepler 22b is the place for you. The brochure has it otherwise, of course. I glance across at Karen's copy. She pretends to read it, playing with her hair at the same time, the way that women do when they grow bored.

I study the back cover between intense glances at an unreachable finishing point, which is also the location of our hotel. It displays an advert for an estate of empty apartments overlooking an as yet unnamed lake that I happen to know is more than three times the size of anything on Earth. So, there is water, somewhere.

Almost twenty years on from Kepler's first settlement, there's already been a property crash. We were here out of intrigue, if nothing else, and because Karen's Dad had bankrolled most of the eye-wateringly priced transportation.

"I'll pay him back," she'd said, the way people do when they borrow money from their parents that they never pay back.

I didn't know if she was also talking about my half of the money. I'd have to churn out a hell of lot of travel writing in order to pay him back the cash. And, knowing his reputation, I'd have to do it fast if I didn't want gaffer-taping to an anvil and lobbing in the River Tees.

Every few minutes the Dust Bus emits a jet of air from somewhere above my head to facilitate blinking. It's easy to forget to blink because there's nothing to do with your eyes other than point them in the direction you're going in. The Dust Bus is so state-of-the-art, you don't even need to drive it, but I do anyway because I don't trust technology. There's nothing to crash into… no plants… no wildlife… no overpriced petrol stations… but I hope to find something. We're running on batteries and electricity from lightning storms, according to the promotional guff I read on the flight... 'The Greatest Show Off Earth' it proclaimed, of Kepler's natural features. It failed to mention the 42 'lightning harvesters' who were electrocuted in the midst of one of the storms a few weeks ago. This then is mankind's last travel experience: cruising the fjords, heli-skiing across the Alps, charred to a cinder sun-worshipping in the Maldives, drinking your own weight in whatever they're passing off as vodka in Magaluf these days. Such earthly pleasures are now *passé*. Interplanetary travel is *it*. A three-day flight in what is effectively a kerosene-powered roman candle, to the outlying satellite planet of Kepler 22, which is a star, then onto our hotel, on Kepler 22b. 22 is fast becoming the modern equivalent of 1960s Goa, with hipsters, if they can be called such a thing when it costs $24,000 per person to even get there, hoping to drop out somewhere off the main trail. Even space travel has gone mainstream. Outside of the confines of the Kepler 22 transport hub is unknown territory, so, if you're garrotted by a triffid or anally probed by an ET-esque index finger, you're unlikely to be covered by any insurance policy.

There's no natural foliage, or wildlife, to speak of on 22b so, outside of the hotel complex at least, you're restricted to a teenage gamer's diet of freeze-dried, powdered everything: noodles, vegan beef jerky... unique in its beeflessness, Angel Delight, Smash, and Hula Hoops. Astronaut food, essentially. I was disappointed to learn that nothing floats, as a lifetime of science fiction books and films had led me to believe, and that it was the second coldest place I've ever been to. After Blackpool in April.

The Dust Bus radio plays only classical music, either as a nod to Kubrick's 2001: A Space Odyssey, which has shaped almost every perception of space travel, or because it's an advertising company's go-to motif for selling absolutely anything. It's playing Neptune - The Mystic, from Holst's Planets suite, right now. I recognise that particular piece because a friend of mine used to ingest considerable amounts of acid and listen to it whilst lying on his kitchen floor. It's eerie yet relaxing at the same time. The full suite of songs plays on a loop and starts again with Mars - Bringer Of War, reaching its thunderous crescendo as we pull up to the hotel, as though our arrival does indeed herald the 'bringing of war'. I've got a face like thunder and Karen's got her feet on the dashboard as she clips her toenails.

From outside, the hotel looks like it was designed by my friend, full of acid, whilst lying on his kitchen floor. It's a bastard cross between the Club Obi Wan from Indiana Jones and the Temple of Doom, and an X-Scape snowdome. A reminder of winter hardly seems necessary when you're supposed to be on holiday. A permanently overcast sky does not help. It's around 6pm and we are in almost complete darkness. There's no artificial light beyond that provided by the hotel. The stars are as clear and sharp as diamonds, but few and far between, it seems, at first glance.

There's a bust of astronomer Johannes Kepler, the planet's earthly namesake, in the lobby. Disappointingly, the sculptor has underplayed Kepler's moustache, presumably to save on bronze. He had a real twizzler, as did all the lads back in the 17th century. Kepler's pal, Tyco Brahe, and the magnificently named Wacker von Wackenfels, were both impressively moustachioed.

The quote beneath the bust reads:

I measured the skies, now the shadows I measure
Skybound was the mind, earthbound the body rests

My first impression is that the developers have managed to strike a fine balance between automata and human interaction. We're about to check-in with the concierge, one of the few humans we've encountered since arriving, when another guest blunders ahead of us. I already know they're going to be the couple that latches onto us, or that Karen latches onto, for the duration of the trip. She's desperate to interact with anyone other than me for the two long weeks we're here, so why not a couple of brash Texans? Is there any other kind? I know they're from Texas, or at least one of the southern states, before they even speak. He's wearing panelled Carhartt chinos held together at the waistline by a belt buckle that looks like an inverted Fray Bentos tin. With bullhorns.

Karen's bristling with excitement at their apparent exoticism, even though we've travelled to another planet for a holiday... what could be more exotic than that?

They're everything Karen wants us to be... immaculately dentured, rich — judging by their jewellery, and pleased to be on holiday.

"They're probably here to colonise something," I whisper, "or stampede the fuck out of the virgin plains with 600 tonnes of soon-to-be-slaughtered cattle."

Karen hovers on the fringes of their check-in procedure, desperate to be invited in.

The concierge is so bureaucratic that he might as well be a robot... or French! I notice his adherence to hotel regulations is infinite, as he drones through a litany of procedures, whilst the Texans nod along blankly. He's hard to take seriously though, as he's dressed like Virgil Tracy. I'm not sure if this is early days novelty themed-hotel thinking, or that it's the standard for interplanetary tourism now. Despite the formalities there's a certain familiarity to the exchange, as though this isn't the first time they've met.

I can see from the bio-passport in the girl's hand that she's a 27-year-old Capricorn called Emmy. There's a Capricorn One remark floating around in my head but I'm too tired to work it out and offer it up. Karen notices Emmy's shoes, but little else.

There's some issue with their reservation so Chinos leans over the desk to get a look at the concierge's touch screen.

His trousers ride up over white socks and overproduced trainers with big flapping tongues. American, down to his bootstraps.

The concierge looks mortified at the approach and rears back. If we were in Texas he would have whipped out a shotgun and painted the lobby with rocksalt and brain flesh by now. Chinos rocks back down off the counter.

Karen can no longer contain herself. She *must* engage with these people.

"I'm sensing their vibes," she says, "there's an energy about them."

I wince as she pats herself down and checks her hair in her phone screen. I await the opening gambit from a woman who once introduced herself at a job interview as 'Kieran'.

She interrupts, to the consternation of the concierge, who looks like he's just been slapped across the face. He throws a look so powerful that it stuns Karen, and even I, standing behind her, can feel the warmth of its rays.

The couple look around blankly... no smiles, no greetings, nothing. Chinos' eyes don't move. He doesn't even blink. Then they return to the concierge, who by now just wants everybody gone. The issue is resolved and the couple move off quietly.

"That was a bit weird, wasn't it?" Karen says, disappointedly.

"You certainly are."

There's no view to speak of. There's nothing, as far as the eye can see, beyond the immediate grounds of the hotel. This is hugely appealing to me, and I'm itching to get out there and have the skin flayed from my face by a flesh-eating cactus, preferably accompanied by a score from Tangerine Dream.

"You can adjust the windows," Karen points out, fiddling with a control panel that effectively turns the glass into the pastoral scene of your choice, not dissimilar to sitting in your living room and watching the telly. She flicks through a few of the generic screensaver-style options — desert, tropical jungle, apocalyptic dystopia — before settling on a moonscape, which is almost exactly what the natural view is anyway, if it can be called that. There's a robot cleaning the skirting boards. One of them annoying little fuckers that people use to cut the grass. The sort that always gets a chainsaw stuck in it on Robot Wars. It's beeping away, rather annoyingly, but it looks happy in its work, which is more than I can say for any of the human staff I've seen around the place, that — so far — number precisely one.

I open a small cupboard above the bed, expecting to find a Gideon's Bible but instead there's a guidebook concerned only with what might happen to you if you leave the complex without an official tour guide. It's grim reading for anyone who's come on holiday to relax but most of the things described are no worse than encounters I've had in numerous Earthbound hotels and hostels. I once had to use a 'dry' toilet in Lyon.

There's a detailed list of how to survive everything including the frequent electrical storms. Top tip: don't wave your golfclubs in the air, and leave your tinfoil hat at home. One of the gravest sounding threats is something called 'atmospheric asphyxiation' which seems to be instant suffocation, if the diagram is anything to go by, and could happen at any time.

The communal areas of the hotel complex are peculiarly artificial. An 'eternal day', as someone I overheard on the flight put it, is the creation of daylight in the surrounding gardens and pool area that eviscerates the permanent darkness lurking on the edge of it. As the journey from spaceport to hotel was in the dark, I equated it to be around 6pm, or approximately the present nightfall equivalent on Earth. The journey from Earth had taken four days. No one here seems to even know, or care, if it's day or night. The long-term staff, the inhabitants, are of either a deathly complexion, or marmalade orange, with seemingly no in-between. I'm at the paler end of the scale, as you might expect. The temperature around the pool area, where we spend our first full day, is in keeping with a holiday atmosphere, settling at around 28 degrees, but is completely fabricated, along with the lighting. Beyond the hotel boundary, it is pitch black. I have to get into that darkness, and the very idea of it seizes me when I'm supposed to be relaxing by the pool. I'm not wholly comfortable with the poolside set up. We're laid out on recliners, our skin cooking under artificial light like marijuana plants in a council house loft.

The atmosphere around the pool is unusual. Nobody's talking, which suits me fine, but the most striking thing of all is that nobody bats an eyelid when Karen casually strips completely naked in full view of everyone. She's discreet enough about it, unclasping her bikini and slipping off the matching bottoms, before lying face down on her recliner. Without going into too much detail, she's in what I would call 'holiday shape' and she, and countless advertising twats, would call 'beach ready'. Her gold-white stomach's as flat as a tile and her arse is like a copper bronze. Her hair's tied back in a ponytail, she's wearing a pair of enormous sunglasses, and absolutely nothing else.

A waiter passes – a human! – and barely glances at her. Other guests, mainly couples, don't respond. I can't tell if I'm glad or annoyed about it. I'm still thinking about what's over that fence. I decide to make my own investigations, tonight, whenever, or whatever, night actually is.

"Are you coming or what?" I say to Karen, as I pack my bag. I suddenly realise that I don't know what I'm packing for. What do I need? A ray gun and an emergency Twix?

'You shouldn't really go off the site. Have you seen all the stuff in that booklet?" she shudders.

"I'm from Spencerbeck," I say, sternly. "I don't think a little green man is going to cause me too many problems."

She rolls her eyes.

"Did you notice around the pool, earlier, when you

stripped off, nobody so much as looked up. What's all that about?"

"What are you trying to say?"

I roll my eyes.

"Well, it's weird, innit? You're stripping off in full view and nobody looks up."

"Did you look up when everyone else's girlfriend stripped off?"

"Of course not."

"Well, there you go, then."

"Well, that was the weird thing. None of them were really sunbathing, anyway. Most of them were covered up. Daft arse still had his chinos on."

"How did you know they were mostly covered up if you weren't really looking at them, then?"

"I'm going," I say. "Are you coming or not?"

The concierge from yesterday is back on duty, as we walk through the foyer.

"There are no tours at this time, sir," he says firmly, as we approach the main doors.

"It is advisable to stay on the site," he adds.

"See," Karen says, clutching at my arm.

"Advisable, not obligatory," I say.

The concierge adds nothing further but, in the reflection of my phone screen as we exit the lobby, I notice him activate his headset telephone and begin speaking to someone. He cranes forward over the counter slightly and looks in our direction.

I watch him again in the rear view mirror of the Dust Bus as we pull away. He is at the main doors.

"There's only one road," Karen points out, as we leave the carpark, "back towards the airport."

"Where we're going, we don't need roads, baby," I shout, swinging the car into a sharp right and veering out of the single lane.

The vehicle suddenly shuts down. We skid to a jolting stop, as if I've stalled it.

"You've stalled it, you tit," Karen says.

"I haven't." I fiddle with the thumbprint panel, trying to restart it. There's nothing doing. I look back and can still see the hotel.

The car powers back into action without me doing anything further. It commences to reverse all the way back to the hotel... a strangely unique and emasculating experience for a male driver. Here I am, being dragged backwards, with no control over it whatsoever. I don't know how, but the Dust Bus activated itself without my thumbprint, which is a revelation as everything on the whole planet requires a thumbprint.

Kepler: It's A Big Thumbs Up From Me. There's a slogan for the tourist board, right there.

Don't bother coming unless you've got your own thumbs. Or at least somebody else's who's already been, like when you give your Beamish Museum ticket away because you're not going to be going again in the next twelve months.

We are now moving backwards at fifteen miles an hour on this inverted road trip.

The Dust Bus dumps us back in the carpark.

The concierge looks as smug as ever.

"Oi, pal, what's that all about?" I say, back inside, ironically jerking a thumb at the carpark.

"Organised trips only, sir. I did say." It's at this point I realise he has no placeable accent. Always a massive danger sign. He isn't from *anywhere*.

"It's not safe, sir."

"I've just been driven backwards at 20mph for almost a mile, mate," I say.

"A mile, sir?" he says, quizzically.

"A Kepler mile," I emphasise, loudly, losing my patience.

"The ways are different here, sir. For your own safety. It's all in the…"

I cut him off, "Yeah, yeah, the guidebook."

"I told you," says Karen, unhelpfully.

"Okay. So, I'm not in control of the vehicle and it's being dragged backwards and someone smashes me arse-end in. What's safe about that?"

"*Arsend*, sir?" he says, mulling over the words.

"The back of the car," I say, louder this time.

"No accidents on Kepler, sir. Nothing to trouble yourself with there, sir."

I hate being called 'sir'. This riles me even more.

"So, we can't leave?"

"Organised tours only, sir. None this evening, though."

"What if I need to get to the airport in an emergency?" I ask.

"No emergencies on Kepler, sir."

"Oh, this bloke's a real piece of work," I say to no one particular.

Karen shunts me off to the room.

"I'll thumb a lift back next time, mate. Don't worry about it," I add as a parting shot.

"Well, we've had a run out," I say, as we step into the lift. "I need a drink."

"You wanna chill out first, don't you," she says, as I bite into the emergency Twix.

"We'll go down to that piano bar," I suggest.

"I need to get changed first," she says, even though we've only been out of the room for half an hour, if that.

I give her a sarcastic thumbs up.

The concierge is working as the barman. Of course he is. He doesn't really serve any drinks, instead instructing you to sort yourself out using your thumb... what else? There's another one for the tourist board, right there: *Sort yourself out using your thumb.*

Even the entertainment is self-service. At various points along the bar, and on the tables in the seating pods, are digital projections of piano keyboards that respond to the touch, just like normal keyboards. I plonk a few keys, but stop when Karen gives me the sort of look I've previously received from the concierge, who I am now referring to as 'Serge', in acknowledgement of his Gallic manner, for my own amusement.

My musical endeavours are displayed on a large plasma screen behind the bar, in the form of a Guitar Hero-style run of chords that respond to your attempts to play. This serves to inform everyone how badly you can play a piano both aurally, and visually. Not that many people are around to see or hear it, barely a handful of guests, none that I recognise from poolside yesterday, but who are all wearing sunglasses.

We order some drinks and remain at the bar. I want to get a handle on what Serge's game is.

"Wearing your bartending hat, tonight," I say, by way of provoking some small talk.

"Excuse me, sir?"

He hardly ever responds to anything without first saying 'excuse me, sir' as though he doesn't know what you're talking about.

"You're working behind the bar tonight," I reiterate.

"Yes, sir. Of course."

"You don't have to call me 'sir'," I say, at which he gives a closed-lipped smile and turns away briefly.

"This whole place is intriguingly weird," I say, turning to Karen.

"Yeah, it is a bit, innit?" she says. "Wonder why?"

"I think it's because they're all robots. Or at least androids."

"Haha, yeah," she agrees, jokingly, then notices I'm serious.

Which I am.

"Are you serious?" she says.

"I am, yeah. Totally. Think about it. Everyone is fully-automated. No one laughs. No one smiles. No one even pervs on YOU," I lech.

She peals off a giggle then notices that Serge is watching us.

He hasn't moved for at least five minutes. I've worked in a bar. You might spend thirty seconds or so propped up against the back bar having a breather, or busy yourself with cleaning glasses, and tidying up. Not Serge. He doesn't move. He doesn't even lean on anything. He barely even blinks. He just stands stock straight, looking out across the bar. He remains in position until a new customer enters.

"Here's Chinos," Karen says, looking over my shoulder.

I pull off my personal best eye roll time.

"Has he got his chinos on?"

She howls again, loud enough to draw him and Emmy over to us.

We exchange some excruciatingly awkward pleasantries, in the middle of which Karen manages to babble the entire story of the amazing backwards Dust Bus.

To add to the absurdity of the whole holiday, Chinos, who on closer inspection I notice has something of the Italian in him, announces himself as Dino.

I draw in my lips, trying not to show any reaction, and look directly at Karen, who appears to be resisting the urge to wet herself with mirth. Her eyes are beginning to water slightly, as she stifles it.

I'm deadpanning it out, as usual, when Karen suddenly

blurts out, by way of explanation, that her 'contact lenses are playing up'.

She doesn't wear contact lenses. She dabs her eyes and composes herself. The conversation goes to next level batshit when Dino tells us that he's an optometrist. It's his polite way of saying 'Karen, love, you're full of shit', which is what I've wanted to say to her for years but have never quite known how without my own eyes turning forty shades of black and blue.

"From the Lone Star State, huh, Dino?" I say, sounding like an absolute bloody bloke.

"Sure," he says. "How'd you guess?"

"I noticed the ol' belt buckle," I say.

"You looking at Chinos' groin area?" Karen says, jokingly, pulling a face. She's half-cut, now. Neither Dino or Emmy respond as they're chatting to Serge, who still hasn't blinked.

"He's called Dino," I say to Karen, quietly.

"Whatever," she replies.

"Has this guy got something wrong with him?" Dino asks discreetly, referring to Serge, who has returned to his mannequin-like pose.

"Diiino," Emmy says, "don't be rude."

"He, like, hasn't blinked once. I can see how dry his eyes are from here."

"Thank you," I say, smugly.

"I don't mean to talk shop with y'all," Dino continues, "but I tend to notice things when it comes to eyes."

You'd notice if someone said they wore contact lenses when they didn't, I think to myself.

"I don't know what the game is there, mate," I say, "or anywhere else on this planet."

"We're here two, maybe three times a year," Dino says, looking to Emmy for confirmation. "For work. What line of work you in?"

I tell him I'm a travel writer, which I suppose I am, even though I'm on holiday, but there's no holiday from writing, and I'm reminded how pretentious it sounds, even though I've been at it for almost twenty years.

I'm glad he's not impressed by it, in the way that most people are. Like most Texans, his favourite subject is himself so I let him fly. He runs a multi-million dollar company called Thumb Luck, which is responsible for the technology that ultimately controls Kepler, through thumbprint recognition.

"I was in the right place at the right time," he says, of the explosion of investment around twenty years ago when it became clear that Kepler was going to be a holiday destination, and not just another squabbled over toy or scientific project for global governments.

"I'm always looking to expand," he continues. "The thumbprint thing is kinda over, now. It's easily exploited, but I guess you heard about that."

"No. I didn't."

"Well, it was kinda kept out of the press, I guess. Hey, another round?"

"Sure," I say, "I think Karen's…"

"Heeey, you guys talking about me?" Karen bursts in. She never says 'guys'. I think Emmy's infected her.

"More drinks," she says, loudly, and, "wooo." She's drunk, now, but we're all on our way.

Serge powers up and prepares a round, the same again, looking peeved that we're not using the self-service system.

"So, now, it's all about optics, which is totally my thing," Dino says.

"So, that's the future around here?" I ask.

"Yeah, sure is. Retinal scanning. It's safer than thumbs."

"How?"

"A guy, well, a bunch guys, I guess, were going around hacking off folks' thumbs and using them to access various places. Government buildings. Hotels. All kinds of stuff. Over at 2-SITE."

"What's 2-SITE?" I ask.

"Other side of the island, or planet, rather, whatever you wanna call it." He takes a swig from his drink.

"There's other resorts?" I ask.

"Not really resorts, but certainly bases, for storage, and staff residential living, if you can call it that."

"Where?"

"It's a long way out. I did some work there. You can't get there. If you try to, they'll talk you out of it, or…"

"Or override your car," I interrupt.

"Yeah. Same thing as happened to you guys, I guess."

"Have you been?" I continue.

"Sure. Did some work on my new projects there. There's lots, heaps, of security clearance required."

Emmy shuffles over. "Honey, I hope you're not giving away 2-SITE secrets," she says, smilingly and rubbing Dino's arm.

I feel the need to compete with this affection and lean over to kiss Karen. I'm watching Serge over her shoulder as I do so. Still nothing. Karen is hammered by now, and I'm starting to feel woozy.

"Y'know, why don't you guys come up to our room?" Emmy says suddenly.

There's no time to answer in the negative as Karen has already loudly accepted the invitation. I'm intrigued to hear more about 2-SITE and if it means we have to throw our car keys, or thumbs, as is more likely, into a bowl and swap partners, then so be it.

The room is the best of it as far as the hotel is concerned.

"You can control the lights by blinking, if you want to," Emmy says, as she thumbs us through the door.

"Don't invite Serge, then," I say, "you'll be sat in the dark all night."

"Baziiing," Karen shouts, loudly enough to startle everyone, especially me, as I've never heard her use the term before.

"Who's Serge?" Dino says.

"The waiter," I say. "We started calling him 'Serge' because I said he reminded me of some French bureaucrat."

"That's Greg," Emmy says. "Nice guy."

"Yeah, a bit weird, though, maybe," I say.

"Greg. Greg. Gregory. Gregor. Gregarious," Karen says, riffing on the name in her drunkenness.

"You're pissed, you," I say.

"What about?" Emmy asks.

"Huh?" I shrug and admire the room.

"What's she pissed about?"

"Oh," I say, "pissed as in drunk, I mean. You guys say pissed for when someone's angry, right?"

I notice that the room, probably two or three times the size of ours, contains various internal doors. It isn't just a room, it's a suite of rooms.

We sit around with more drinks, small talking in the humid air produced and controlled entirely from a control panel projected onto a white ceramic coffee table between the four of us.

"He came up here, once. For a drink," Dino says.

"Who?" Karen replies.

"Greg."

"Oh, right."

"He was helping us out with a thing, wasn't he, hun?" Emmy says.

"Sure. Say, Karen, you've got beautiful eyes," Dino says, and then, turning to me, "I hope you don't mind me a paying a compliment."

I think this is the bit where we all go to bed together.

"I would love to have eyes like yours," Emmy says, leaning in closer to Karen.

"Me too," Dino agrees, "sure are pretty."

"The best I've seen on Kepler," Emmy adds.

"Is there a particular type of 'eye' around here?" I laugh.

Dino and Emmy glance at each other.

"Dino does a lot of 'cosmetic' work around here. He's a qualified surgeon, and we figured that, as this is now a holiday destination, he might pick up some work on the tourists. Kinda like a Palm Springs dentist or something."

"What sort of work?" Karen asks, coming back to life.

"There's a kinda situation here on Kepler," Dino begins to explain, piquing my interest. "Even though it's been open to tourists for twenty years, it was inhabited by contractors closer to forty years ago, when work first began on colonisation. Many of them settled here, as much as you can settle, or stayed on, you might call it and reproduced... as you do. That second generation are now the natives, if you like, but they've never adapted to the light, or lack of it. Slowly, over half a century or so, their eyesight has deteriorated rapidly. They are being slowly blinded."

I'm open-mouthed, as I remember the lack of poolside interest in Karen, and Serge's seeming inability to blink.

He was helping us out with a thing.

"Dino's here to help those people," Emmy says, attempting to assuage mine and Karen's shock.

A private American healthcare company is *here to help*.

She continues, "He does 'transfers', don't you, honey?"

"Sure, honey," he replies. "I've developed a technique where I can effectively carry out eye transplants."

I give a long, slow blink.

"There's a demand. For eyes. I can meet that demand."

"What. The. Fuck?" I say.

"I know it's kinda weird," Dino says, "but it's a burgeoning procedure that I'm a master of."

"Assuming this is actually real…" I say, questioning everything inside my head, "where do you get the 'new eyes' from?"

"Tourists," he says, matter-of-factly.

"We call them 'Earth eyes', don't we, honey?" Emmy says, smiling.

"You listening to this?" I say to Karen.

"$12,000 per eye is the current going rate," he offers.

"So you put the tourists' eyes IN the Keplerian's eye sockets?"

"Sure do."

I let out a small burst of laughter.

"It's a two-day procedure. Don't feel a thing."

"Well, that's reassuring," I say, dryly.

"What do you do with the 'old eyes'?" I ask.

"I take care of them, at, at…"

"2-SITE?" I interrupt.

"There's means of disposal," he says, "although I'm something of a hoarder."

I venture no further into that remark.

"I can't believe I'm asking this, but what do you replace the human eyes with?"

"A fully-working synthetic piece. An ocular prosthetic, if you will. There are degrees of maintenance involved, as you'd expect. Back on Earth, no one will even notice."

Karen is finishing another drink. I don't know if she's even listening.

"Whole procedure takes place right here," Dino says, pushing the line and gesturing at one of the closed internal doors, "clean, sterile environment, probably more so than many hospitals back on Earth."

"Serge," I say, "I mean 'Greg'...?"

"Yeah, right here."

"He doesn't blink," I say, "never."

"Needs some minor adjustments. Ongoing maintenance, you might say. Our aftercare is first rate," Dino says, inspecting the palms of his hands as if he's about to start the procedure right away. He breaks eye contact with me when he mentions 'aftercare'.

He stretches his fingers and squeezes each knuckle in turn.

There's a distinct click sound from the direction of the main door. I remember from our own room that it means the door has been locked remotely.

Emmy is still smiling and refilling our drinks glasses.

He was helping us out with a thing.

"I think we need to go," I say, my vision blurring slightly as I move to stand.

"There's no hurry," Emmy says, pushing our glasses forward in a manner that suggests she *isn't* about to steal our *fucking* eyeballs.

Karen suddenly springs to life. "Wait a minute..."

At last, she senses the potential complications of having your eyeballs removed by a couple of perfect strangers.

She's going to kick off and help me fight our way out of here…

But no. "$12,000 per eye?" she says, sly and calculating, regarding Dino then Emmy. "Is that what Keplerians pay *you* or is that what you pay the *tourists*…?"

"Y'know, there's a saying where I come from," I say to Karen as we load the Dust Bus and set off for the spaceport.

"Oh, yeah. What's that?" she says, adjusting her sunglasses in the rear view, in which, once again, we can see Serge in the hotel doorway.

"If someone thinks they're being lied to, or ripped off, they say, 'Are you having my eyes out?'"

"So what?" she says. "I like these new ones."

GOIN' BACK TO PRESTWICK

Another petrol station, brilliant green and white neon lights, the same soulless selection of damp, day-old pasties, and the monotonous soundtrack of passing traffic. It was worse by night, perhaps magnified by the low ambience, but there were less people around – a good thing. The rest rooms throbbed with the day's mephitis; the smell of function. The plink and zap of frugal fruit machines.

He couldn't remember – on hearing that music – when he first told himself that he wasn't going to work for anybody, that nobody was going to be his boss. He thought about it as he pulled on the handbrake and reached for the bag on the passenger seat, his lower back creaking and jarring. He knew all the terminology by now: 'L1 to 5' 'sacrum' 'gibbus' – all damaged by the gyrating and the hard miles. His walk: slow, confident. The head bobbing to a slow internal rhythm. He hoped the bathroom was empty. Few people around: the occasional worker slipping out for a cigarette, a lorry driver leaning against the heavy tarp screen of his vehicle, beneath the name 'L.C. Humes Haulage'.

Just after 8pm on an autumn evening; cold enough to see your breath. A quick look around. Was it familiar? He didn't know anymore. Was it new? Maybe he had been here before. His memory was weaker now; with age, everything looked the same.

Inside, he saw the 'Colonel' selling chicken. Stale Hawaiian pizza, re-cooking nicely beneath white light and grubby glass. At the bathroom, he pushed open the door and revelled in the emptiness of his surroundings. Three grim sinks, five smeared taps, and a flickering dull bulb to illuminate the wider-with-every-inspection bald patch. As a dressing room, it wasn't the worst he had seen. He placed the bag beside the sink and leaned into the mirror – into himself, whoever 'himself' now was.

"The image is one thing and the human being is another…"

It was all there… the parched skin, the heavy jowls, the eyes dry from the long hours on the roads. How long could he do this for? *Another* 25 years? He felt he could barely get to where he was headed now.

The flashing light worsened his headache. He opened the bag and took out the box. He knew how it worked but read through the instructions anyway, with a wincing inner embarrassment. He removed the bottle, and the lid, and doused the contents through a stainless steel comb. The comb sliced through whatever was left up there. It would be passable, in half an hour or so, with a bit of committed sprucing and careful attention to the roots.

He slicked it back with his open palm, feeling the shine and glide as the years fell away. In the mirror he saw his lip curl involuntarily and eyebrow arching without prompt. He was changing.

Onward then: North. Another 20 miles. Maybe more.

"It's on the coast, son. Freeman's Hall. Glenbaairrn Road," barked the man on the phone a few weeks earlier, from somewhere in Scotland, he deduced from the accent.

Prestwick Masonic Lodge. A strip-lit kitchen barely big enough for two. The detritus of village life littering the formica worktops: parish newsletters, a stack of paper plates and napkins, a plastic Jesus in white robes nailed to the wall. His own suit hung on the same wall. Tighter now, he thought, as he lifted down this shroud and sucked in the middle-aged gut at the same time. He stepped into the pantsuit, grew three feet taller. The belt clipped across the stomach, like an astronaut locking in for launch. Bone white from toes to teeth – a half-smile peeping out from the side of the mouth.

Metamorphosing now, as the backing track swelled up in the front of house – Ronnie Tutt's Vegas paradiddle engulfing the hall like a swarm of wasps, the rhythm section completed by Jerry Scheff's fat-back bass. In the kitchen, across his front, the blue peacock, and the tinder of chest hair. The burnished bling of 'TCB' over the knuckles, and the final touch – sunglasses, Neostyle Nautics.

Out through the kitchen door and beyond the musty curtain.

Key of A major.

All ages out front. Old enough to know first time round. The Junkie XL crew, and younger still. He rolled on the drum motif. The dye had taken. The quiff had held. He was him now. Everybody knew it; he was lean, slender. The suit cut to the waistline; collar popped high. The voice dropped an octave, controlled by confidence.

He used it all. The Cairo residency. The nights with the showgirls at the conferences in Nevada. The expensive voice coaching. The mockery from his friends when he started out. It all passed through the pages of his mind. On through the set: Ray Charles, Tony Joe White, then slower towards a brief interval. A few of those napkins across the brow back in the kitchen, his pallor now as white as his suit. A clammy fistful of tablets, reds, greens and blues, to fire the circuits again, sloshed along with tepid tap water. Breathing shallow but on with the show. A couple of Beatles numbers, more Ray Charles, and the song he had finished every single set with. He must have sung it well over a thousand times. Then back behind the curtain once more, as the audience shuffled out amongst the scraping plastic chairs and cloakroom hubbub.

He felt the cold porcelain of the toilet against his exposed back, the suit pulled down to his waist. His ventricles thinning out and stretched now; the valves not opening properly. The beat of the music, and his heart, almost gone. His left arm seized, then grabbed with the right; forward, onto his knees, the slaked black hair flattened between forehead and floor. The dye smeared the cold tiles. Blood from the nose on impact, somehow darker than the dye... then nothing.

In the main hall, someone unqualified disconnecting the PA, flicking switches and pressing buttons. It fired again, the CD skittered through a song, and the speakers came alive...

THE DEVIL AND THE FARMER

The farm track was long, straight and flat. You could see anyone coming from the window of the house. The Devil trudged towards it, panting, and grumbling to himself, mainly about the weather, but also the length of the track, the mud and stones in his hooves and the barking dogs at the house. He could see a downstairs light on, and one in the room directly above. The farmer and his wife getting ready for bed, he thought. The Devil knocked on the front door of the farmhouse and dusted off his thighs as he awaited a response. After what the Devil supposed was around thirty seconds, the sound of locks being unbolted cracked the silence of the night air. The dogs had fallen quiet, much to the Devil's relief. The door swung open, sharply. The farmer filled the doorframe, looking as perturbed as the Devil, wearing only his underwear and holding a double-barrel shotgun.

"The fucking Devil," the farmer sighed. "How original."

"Can I come in?" the Devil said, then quickly afterwards, "I'm coming in," without waiting for a reply.

"If you're covered in shit, you can wipe your feet first. Or whatever they are."

"I will. I will," promised the Devil as he stepped into the house.

The farmer lowered his shotgun.

"What do you want, anyway? It's gone ten o'clock."

"Yeah, I know," the Devil said. "I'm freezing. Anyway, I'm doing the rounds, aren't I? All the farms and what have you. Aren't you scared of me? I *am* the Devil, y'know."

The farmer laughed as he ushered the Devil into the kitchen.

"Look, mate," he said, "this morning I dropped a telly on our lass's foot. You should have fucking heard her. I'm surprised you didn't. And the face on her. Jesus Christ. Can I mention him in front of you? Anyway, she hit the fucking roof."

"You can say what you like," the Devil said, regarding the farmer's blasphemy, "it's your house."

"You'll be wanting a drink," the farmer said, reaching into a cupboard.

"I will, yeah," the Devil said, noisily dragging a chair from under the kitchen table.

The farmer's wife bellowed from upstairs, "What the bloody hell's going on, Cliff?"

"Cliff...?" the Devil spluttered, "proper farmer's name, that."

"It's the Devil," the farmer shouted, into the emptiness of the hallway, "he's just called in. He's doing the rounds."

"Is he wearing a watch?" came the voice from upstairs.

"What?" answered the farmer, puzzled.

"Is he wearing a watch?"

Louder, this time.

The farmer shrugged at the Devil.

The farmer's wife again, "If he's not, tell him it's nearly half past fucking ten at night."

"See what I mean?" said the farmer quietly.

"She sounds like a big heavy cow," chuckled the Devil, equally quietly, as he ruffled the fur on his head.

The farmer did not hear him. He was still rummaging through the cupboard. He began to reel off the available drinks, his voice muffled by the acoustics of the cupboard.

"Beer. Gin, that's hers. Wine. A bit of vodka. Advocaat."

"My name's Cliff and I drink Advocaat," the Devil mocked. "I'll have the vodka."

The farmer ignored him and placed two tall glasses on the table.

"You don't look like a farmer," said the Devil.

"You don't look like the Devil," the farmer said.

"I don't look like the Devil!" He was almost offended. "I've got hooves, for fuck's sake." He gestured at his legs, "...and a tail." He swished the latter over the wooden floorboards. "Seen the dirt on that?" he said, inspecting the end of his tail.

"You look like Mr Tumnus," the farmer said, "that little fanny out of er... er... the wotsit?"

"Narnia," the Devil said, clicking his hooves trying to remember, "and them annoying kids. Aaaah, what did they call it?"

"Can't remember," the farmer said, placing down the drinks on the table. "I read it when I was a kid."

"I bet you were expecting someone in human guise, weren't you?" the Devil said.

"I wasn't expecting anyone at this time of night," the farmer replied.

"Like Bulgakov's 'Devil' in his daft book," the Devil continued, "or Al Pacino in the one where he's a lawyer. An everyday bloke who happens to be the Devil. I'm sick of being misrepresented for personal gain, come to think of it. Especially popstars. Cliff Richard. Remember that one? Devil Woman?" He hummed the melody to himself. "Just the other day, my nephew came to me and said, 'Listen to this, Uncle Nick, and it's some record called Devil Said Dance by erm... I forget now. It'll come to me. Anyway, it's not like that. It's like this: cloven hooves and matted fur. I'm supposed to be some sort of animal, aren't I?"

"Like a faun," the farmer laughed, draining his glass. "How come you're wearing a coat anyway?"

"I pinched it from lost property at the bus station," the Devil explained. "I'm used to a warmer climate, remember."

"You came on the bus?" the farmer asked.

"Of course I did. Do you know how many times I get stopped driving a car?"

"Don't the people on the bus bother you?"

"Not really. I think it was the drunk bus. Probably thought they were hallucinating or something. It is nearly Halloween."

"I suppose," said the farmer. "What do you mean by 'you don't look like a farmer'?"

"I thought you were all big fat, greedy, ruddy-faced cunts," the Devil said, unapologetically.

The farmer was quite the opposite.

"You look like James Coburn," the Devil added.

"I suppose it's the same as me expecting you to be in human form," the farmer mused, pouring himself another large drink.

"You are a greedy, heavily-subsidised cunt, though," the Devil snipped, pointing at his own meagre measure. The farmer reluctantly reached for the bottle again as the Devil grinned and played with his glass.

"What's with the accent, anyway?" the farmer asked.

"My parents are from Bristol," the Devil said.

"Thought I detected a bit of Midlands in there somewhere, but maybe not," the farmer said. "So, you said you were checking up on things?"

"Yeah, we need more staff," the Devil said. "Y'know. Down there." He pointed at the area of the floor immediately beneath him.

"Hell?" the farmer said.

"Hell," said the Devil.

"I thought you'd be overcrowded these days," the farmer said, "what with all these politicians and old TV presenters."

"We are in some places, but not in others. We're running low on Catholic priests for the first time since I've been in charge."

"Can't you shuffle people around a bit?" the farmer asked. "Shunt a few of the middle-management arseholes sideways, something like that?"

The Devil let out a deep laugh.

"Let me give you an idea of how things work," he said. "We have various people working in different departments. Years ago, people went wherever I put them. But now. Well, I don't know what goes on up here anymore, but by the time I get hold of them, they won't do a thing you tell them to. Especially the politicians."

"They're like that up here," the farmer interrupted. "They're as thick as pigshit, to a man."

"And the footballers," the Devil started up again, "they think they own the place, parading around in fucking sandals and socks... in those temperatures. What's that all about? Fuck knows what it'll be like in fifty years' time."

"You'll still be there, won't you?" asked the farmer.

The Devil finished his drink and loudly slammed the glass on the table.

"Will I fuck? I'll be gone in four years."

"Really?" said the farmer. "What happens then?"

"Then I put my hooves up."

"No. I mean who'll be in charge?"

"We're still interviewing. It's a very long process. Takes ages. I like Tony Blair. He's got the two most important qualities for being the Devil."

"What are they?"

"A shifty-as-fuck face and bags of charm. Who'd have thought it from a Socialist?"

"He's as much a Socialist as I'm a bloody ice skater," the farmer spat.

"Let's have one more," said the Devil, reaching for the bottle.

The farmer snatched it away.

"I'll see to that," he said. 'Sounds fucked up down there.'

"Fucked up down there? You've had a Nazi Pope, haven't you?"

"True."

"Actually, he's in the running. The committee like him over Blair."

"You can have him," said the farmer. "We've got a new one now. And the one before him looked like thingy off the darts."

"Wouldn't know," said the Devil.

They drank silently for a few seconds.

"Gadaffi. We're seeing him soon, for the job, once he's cleaned himself up," the Devil said, breaking the silence.

"He's been dead for years. How does that work?" the farmer asked.

"Purgatory, for however long, then on to us."

"Isn't purgatory a Catholic thing?"

"We take what we can get down there, at the minute. He'll need some sorting out, though. Dragged through the streets like a scarecrow version of Michael Jackson, the mad fucker."

"Aye," nodded the farmer. "Anyone else you fancy?" he enquired.

"Cowell. We all like him. Got a sort of mass appeal thing going on, but with a bit of villainy. Few years left in him, though. And we like the show."

"The Devil watches the X-Factor? I've heard it all

now," groaned the farmer, as the Devil crossed his arms in an 'x' shape.

"Every week. Me, Jimi Hendrix, the Marquis de Sade, and the bloke who invented the shellsuit. We all tune in."

The farmer was stunned. "Jimi Hendrix went to Hell?"

"He turned up one day with his guitar and asked to stay cos the Devil has all the best tunes. Dunno where he'd been until then but I wasn't gonna turn him away. Before that, we had to listen to Sid Vicious and his three fucking chords."

"What do you do for fun down there?" the farmer asked, the questions coming fast to his mind now the vodka had started to buzz his system.

"We had a snooker table, which was taken out due to, shall we say, funding issues."

"Such as?"

"Well," said the Devil, "I was constantly losing money to Alex Higgins. Un-fucking-beatable, I'm telling you."

"I can believe it," said the farmer, and then, "what about the women? You never mentioned any."

"Oh, there's loads of them. We all get together on a Sunday and fornicate. They're not just there for that, of course. Everyone just does their own thing."

"I thought you were gonna say that you make them do all the cleaning and tidying up," the farmer laughed.

"Nah," the Devil said. "Hell is considered frightfully liberal to most new arrivals. It's actually woke as fuck."

"I don't know what that is," the farmer said.

"It's like the Guardian's idea of Utopia, except the

temperature is off any global warming scale you might have up here."

"The fucking Guardian," harrumphed the farmer. "Anyway... about the women. Every Sunday, you said?"

"Every Sunday," confirmed the Devil.

"Is... is... Jane Russell there?" the farmer said, sheepishly.

"Yep."

"She... er... still wear them sweaters?"

"Yep."

"I'll get my coat," said the farmer.

THE HEADHUNTERS

"Hello. Is that Horace?"

"Speaking. The Reverend Horace Waterston. Grintle parish. Also, Bishop of Pulney. And..." There was a long suspense-making pause that created scarce little suspense. I let him finish.

"Open hearts, open minds, open doors and all that," he went on.

Great. I'd snagged myself a Methodist. He was still going.

"And... for my sins," he gave a brief chuckle, "Chairman of Grintle Griffins Rugby Union FC. Club secretary. Actually, doubling as."

I was about to speak.

On he went.

"The other fellow's on holiday so I'm taking care of all the er... the er... the day-to-day running, etcetera."

A rugger bugger, as well.

"I'm ringing about Oliver," I said.

"Ah, yes," he said, "let me guess. Newcastle? The famous Geordie accent."

I squeezed my temples with my right hand.

"A bit further south," I said, "but never mind. Now, about the 'head'..."

"Now, wait. Wait." Another pause. "Sunderland?"

"Er… Middlesbrough" I said, correcting him.

"Musselburgh?"

"Middlesbrough. Anyway. The 'head'. I'm an… er… enthusiast. A writer, actually. I'm writing about…"

"Yes. I still have it," he interrupted, confidently.

"Yes," I said, "I'd like to see it."

"Of course. Let us make the necessary arrangements." We duly did.

"You'll be coming a long way, now. To Worcestershire, I mean."

Who, in the name of all Christ, lives in Worcestershire? What is it? Are Teessiders even allowed there? A stronghold of the House of Stuart, according to some mid-A1 hands-free internet surfing, interrupted sporadically by trying to unwrap an overpriced panini from Barnt Green services.

"Just turn right at Hockley Heath," Horace had said on the phone, seemingly oblivious to the fact that I lived over 200 miles away. "The Lord will guide you."

He lived in Barbourne, as it turned out, a Tory playground in which northerners were boiled in oil until their skin fell off, or they renounced Socialism, whichever came first. There was a huge billboard displaying the beaming mug of MP Robin Walker on the road in, where Horace apparently lived, at the church house. I found him rustling around in the garden, jabbing at a clematis with a pair of secateurs, like a bear scooping honey from a beehive. He was a big unit, as we say in these parts. He gave a disapproving look and raised the secateurs.

It was the Clockwork Orange t-shirt I was wearing.

"Will," he called, affirmatively.

"'Tis I," I replied, for reasons I can't explain. When was the last time you said, 'Tis I' whilst confirming your identity?

"A safe trip, I trust?" he asked. "How are you finding the fair county of Worcester?"

He loudly recited the area motto, which I only recognised as I'd seen it on a sign a few miles back.

"The paninis are a bit steep," I said.

"Excuse me?" he said, cupping his ear with the hand that was holding the secateurs. His chafing brown cords gave off thunderclaps of kinetic energy that rumbled through the garden and on towards the village green.

We stepped beneath the rose trellis that led through the front door into the house.

"It's in the basement," he said, pointing towards a short flight of stone steps. "Not the sort of thing I'd want anyone to catch a glimpse of through the window, now, is it? Being the local vicar and all." He emphasised the word 'vicar'.

He flicked a light switch at the bottom of the steps.

"Ol' Ironsides," he said, "quite a character."

I waited at the foot of the steps for the door to slam behind me and the bolt to slide across, like it does in the movies, but it didn't. Instead, a great swathe of midday sun beamed in as Horace returned from the far side of the room carrying a wooden box. It was bright enough but he manoeuvered an angle-poise lamp into position over the box. When he opened it, I was about as close to royalty as I'd ever been. He was unrecognisable, as you might expect, over 360 years later, but it was him, 'warts and all'.

A shiny dried up shrunken bonce not much bigger than a fist now. There was a splintered stake jammed in the throat from below, from when he'd been displayed above Westminster Hall.

"Ah, well?" said Horace in an attempt to solicit a response.

"Looks like him," I said, "in so far as most people would look after this long. Especially after being booted all over London."

"You're familiar with the provenance?" Horace asked.

"Yeah, I can see where they've sawed the top of his napper off," I said.

"His what, sorry?"

"His 'napper'. His head."

"Ah, yes. Of course. He actually died from malaria, and possible septicaemia. Most people think he was beheaded but that actually took place after his death."

"Less blood that way," I said.

"Indeed," agreed Horace, "perhaps he deserved it."

"Republican," I said, acknowledging myself. "We're talking about a man who was offered the job as king and turned it down. As Englishmen go, that makes him unique, doesn't it?"

"Yes. I suppose it does," mused Horace, drumming his fingers against his lips like George from Rainbow, "but he effectively ruled as king. He lived in the royal palace."

"Meet the new boss," I said, "same as the old boss."

I felt confident that no one had quoted Who lyrics to the Bishop of Grintle before.

"Draped in purple and ermine at his last," the vicar sniped, in a nod to Cromwell's regal funeral. "And so he wasn't beheaded until a couple of years later. Quite remarkable when you think about it. His body was taken to the Red Lion pub in Holborn, then on to Tyburn for the chop."

"I've had a pint in there," I said, "with my mate, Chris. He lives in London." I don't know why I said this. Maybe I was trying to attach myself to the legend of it in some way.

He looked blankly at the head.

"They had to bray fuck out of it to get it off," I said, slipping into my homeland vernacular.

"I beg your pardon?" he said, snapping out of a reverie of sorts.

I rephrased it accordingly.

"It looked over London from the Hall gates, then came down in a storm one night," he continued, "would have been up there for a few years by then."

I looked again at the head. It looked fit to come alive once again, as if imbued by all of our talk.

"As I understand it," I said, "it was thereafter stashed up a chimney?"

"So it's believed," said Horace. "It must have been quite a shock to find it. To see this ghastly appendage come bouncing over the rooftops and into the lanes."

"Yes. No wonder he hid it for the best part of two decades," I said.

"It would have been unrecognisable as Cromwell by the time it turned up in the museum," he said, "but whoever found it in the street obviously convinced the buyer, assuming it was sold."

"I'd pay to see it in a museum," I said. "I once paid to see a plate of fish and chips in Barnsley."

"What?" Horace said.

"I think it's a northern thing," I explained, waving a dismissive hand over the box. "Have you ever been to Middlesbrough?" I asked, on a tangent.

"Whitby, once," he said, "a very long time ago. A wilder people I never saw in my whole life."

I laughed and returned my attention to the box. "So, it's in a museum. A curio," I went on.

"Yes. But not curious enough," said Horace. "It wasn't popular. Nobody came. Next up was a notorious drunkard."

"A man after my own heart," I interrupted.

"Samuel Russell," said Horace. "Despite an almost perpetual inebriation, Russell was not for selling, turning down considerable sums from various potential buyers, instead parading it as a party piece at drinking sessions."

I knew that it had eventually been wrested from Russell by a villainous toymaker by the name of James Cox, who himself flogged it on in some state of disrepair for £7,000 in new money. A king's, or indeed, Lord Protector's ransom.

"It seemed to vanish again at the turn of the 19th century," Horace interjected, "and of course resurfaced amid questions of its provenance in the mid-1800s following Thomas Carlyle's book on Cromwell."

"But then it was interred early in the mid-20th century," I asked, "by your father?"

Horace looked at me. The reverential joviality was gone from his face. His lips were dry.

"*A* head was interred," he said firmly.

"At Sussex College?" I said, doubting myself, and turning back to the head in the box that I thought to be Cromwell.

The cord cut right into the skin beneath my Adam's apple. The pain of blood soon went, evaporated by the end of air. My last breath was deep inside me. He dragged me backwards, showing me the ceiling, all rustic roof beams and sandstone. I knew if my heels left the cold stone floor I was dead, hanged by the cord around my neck. An inch off the floor made no more difference than the 6 foot that Cromwell had been hoisted on the gallows. My eyeballs swam. There was no getting my fingers under the wire. His big pudgy mitts pulled it tighter. My lungs would give up before the skin on his fingers did. He was already cutting in. I was already gripping my car key. I shouldn't think there is anywhere recorded an account of a clergyman's death as 'car key right in the eyeball' so we were both pioneers in that sense.

    I just needed to get somewhere near that big head by simply hoisting my hand, and the key, over my right shoulder. Scrape his forehead. Jab his ear. I got lucky. It went straight into his eyeball, like a cocktail stick through a pickled onion. The mush sprayed over the back of my head. Retina, cornea, snot, blood, all over. He made no sound but he promptly slackened off the ligature. I let go of the key. It had struck with such satisfaction that my original horror was all but gone. We were both going back over now, but only one of us might have been dead by the time Horace's head hit the workbench behind us. His left eye may have blinked as his spinal cord detached at the neck, the last thing it saw being the back of my head falling towards it.

I rolled off him sideways and lay face down on the white floor. The wire had cut deep at the taut points on the side of my neck but I could breathe. I leaned on my elbow and looked at Horace's body. Blood began to pool beneath his head. His right eye was gone, pinned into the back of the socket by the car key, with only a little of the Transporter Bridge novelty keyring protruding, laying against his bloodied cheek like a tattoo. I prized the key from the mess and wiped it in his armpit. I drew myself up to my knees and steadied myself against the bench. My skin was cold, and crawling. There was bile in my throat. I swallowed it down and felt dizzy. The head belonged to me now. I closed the box and turned for the stairs.

I'd parked a short walk from the house. I cleaned the blood from my neck, most of it obscured by my beard, and quietly stepped out beneath the rose trellis. I didn't see anyone on the way back to the car. I placed the box in the boot and drove all the way back to Boro without stopping.

THE ANFIELD MURDER

"He lived as a Devil, eh?"

"Quite. Of course, that doesn't make him a murderer, Sergeant Dewclaw," replied Detective Larsen.

"No, sir. In fact, we can rule him out," Dewclaw said, reluctantly turning a charge sheet over so it lay face down on the detective's desk.

"So, what do we have left?" Larsen mused, loudly, as he pushed his last Senior Service between his lips.

"A timid-as-a-dormouse chess enthusiast who just happens to be the victim's husband, sir."

"Ah, yes. The husband," Larsen said, inspecting the empty cigarette packet.

A Product Of The Master Mind read the slogan across the side.

Indeed, thought Larsen, looking up at the blackboard on the office wall through the first new plume of smoke.

"An insurance salesman, you say?"

"Yes, sir. Somewhat ordinary lifestyle, as you might expect. A teetotal non-smoker."

He gave a sideways glance at the detective's cigarette, which was returned by Larsen.

"Middle-aged," continued Larsen, to no one in particular. "Well-to-do. Somewhat unfulfilled. Aren't we all?" He let the thought hang in the air, then spoke again. "And an alibi as impenetrable as anything I've heard in thirty-four years on the force."

Dewclaw slumped into a chair and puffed out his cheeks. The ribbons of smoke danced away from him towards the window that looked out on to Walton Lane, and further across Anfield.

Not for the first time, Larsen asked, "And there's absolutely no such address as 25 Menlove Gardens East?"

"Absolutely not, sir. Only a Menlove Avenue, which is comprised of only even numbers."

"So," said Larsen, authoritatively, "Wallace, the husband, sets out on foot to his chess group meeting, as he does most weeks, on a Thursday evening."

"That's right, sir," Dewclaw confirmed, now back on his feet and staring hard at the map he had chalked on the blackboard a few days earlier.

Larsen took up the thread again. "Mrs Wallace, as far as we know, is at home, but has been known to accompany him in the past?"

"Yes, sir, but not on this occasion," added Dewclaw.

Larsen firmly positioned an inkwell on his desk with his right hand.

"Wallace's house," he announced.

To his left, he laid down the cigarette packet.

"Chess club," he said.

"About a fifteen minute walk, sir," Dewclaw said.

"He arrives at the chess club, to be told by the… the… Grandmaster, or whoever, that he has received a request to contact a Mr Qualtrough, of whom Wallace claims to have never heard."

"That's right, sir. Neither Wallace nor anyone at the chess club recognises the name, or, perhaps even more importantly, the voice attached to it."

"Local accent?" Larsen asked.

"Local accent."

"Can't say I've ever heard the name," Larsen continued.

"Scottish, sir. Not a single one listed in the area based on any existing records."

Larsen rolled the name on his tongue as he finished his cigarette.

"This Qualtrough, then," he said, "must know that Wallace is a member of the club, or know his routine, which wouldn't be difficult to determine with someone as seemingly unadventurous as Wallace."

"It would appear so, yes, sir."

"And, according to this club captain, the caller requests that Wallace visit him at an address that turns out not to exist. This Menlove Gardens East place?"

"Yes, sir. And adds that he cannot call back later, perhaps by which time Wallace has arrived at the chess club, and can take a call, as he is 'involved in my daughter's 21st birthday celebrations' or so he says, and he doesn't leave a contact number."

The detective stroked his moustache.

"One line of enquiry springs to mind," he said. "Establishing precisely how many local girls celebrated their 21st birthday on... what was the date?"

"January 20th, sir. But who's to say there ever was a birthday party to celebrate?"

"Yes, quite. Another ruse. Could Wallace have made the call himself?"

"A possibility, sir, but his voice would surely have been recognised by the man at the chess club."

"Yes, or he could have arranged for someone else to make the call." He thought for a moment. "Or no call was ever made. A fiction conceived by the man at the chess club."

"The other members distinctly remember him taking the call, and his general bewilderment thereafter. It seems unlikely he would fake this, and, in any case, was at the chess club the following evening when the murder took place."

"Yes, the next night," said Larsen, placing a matchbox at a point a little further east of the inkwell on his desk. "Then Wallace pays a visit to this perfect stranger, as he said he would to the chaps at the chess club, on the basis of this mysterious phone call."

Dewclaw leaned forward and traced a finger between the inkwell and the matchbox.

"He's looking for 25 Menlove Gardens East in the knowledge that there is, at least, a Menlove Avenue in the vicinity," described Dewclaw, "and he's in insurance so you would expect him to have a good knowledge of the local area as a result."

"Whoever has requested his presence wouldn't know if he was coming or not," interrupted Larsen. "No time was specified and it was approximately twenty-four hours later. Someone knows that Wallace is out of the house for a short window of time."

"About fifteen minutes again, sir, but consider additional time searching for a non-existent address."

"And we've no witnesses?" Larsen asked.

"He claims to have asked directions from two people, one of whom can corroborate this."

"Total time away from the house?"

"Less than an hour, sir. Around forty-five minutes, based on the time police were called."

"By Wallace?" Larsen asked.

"That's right, sir. He says in his statement that he instructed Mrs Wallace to lock the door and not to respond to any calls, in person, or even by telephone, until he returned."

"I've spoken to the neighbours myself," Larsen said. "None of them were aware of anything untoward or even noticed Wallace leave or return."

"It's quite a quandary, sir," said Dewclaw, gazing out of the window.

Larsen picked up the crime sheet in front of him.

"Blunt force trauma to the head. No murder weapon. No forced entry. And if every criminal in the land had an alibi like Wallace's, we wouldn't need jails. It poses more questions than it answers."

He threw down the sheet.

"The room, the house, largely undisturbed. Even the chess pieces were undisturbed in any struggle that might have taken place."

"Excuse me, sir?" Dewclaw said, quizzically.

"I say, telephone still in its cradle. Poker still hanging in the coal scuttle. And the pieces still on the board."

"The crime scene photographs, sir. You say there's pictures?"

"Yes, Dewclaw. Grim stuff."

He threw the file across the desk, toppling the empty ink well. Dewclaw gathered up the file before it had even come to rest. He shuffled quickly through it, stopping at a picture of the surrounding area: an armchair, a small table beside it, supporting the chessboard. Another picture. A close-up of the board, its little wooden pieces standing to attention.

"Sir, look..." Dewclaw said, frantically, unfolding his hand drawn map of the surrounding streets.

"What is it?"

Dewclaw laid out the map, highlighted in pencil with the route the suspected killer took, beside the chessboard. The pieces corresponded precisely to the points on the map.

"Black pawn at A6," Dewclaw announced, pointing to the piece then tracing his finger across to C5. "What was the Wallaces' address?" he asked.

"29 Wolverton Street," said the Inspector.

"There it is," Dewclaw continued, acknowledging a white pawn at C5.

"And this piece is the chess club?" Inspector Larsen asked, squinting at the black pawn on A6.

On the map, Dewclaw reached the familiar shape of the Menlove Avenue area, then glanced at the board.

Places F 1-4 were all occupied, as were G 2 and 3, and H2. They formed a neat triangle in the lower right of the board.

The Inspector reached for his cigarettes, as if a nicotine infusion might give his brain a jolt, briefly forgetting that he had already finished his packet.

"There's a piece missing, sir," Dewclaw added, doing a quick count of the pieces he could see in the photographs, "or at least it's not in this picture."

"Someone," Inspector Larsen said, looking for something to do with his hands in lieu of lighting a cigarette, "is trying to tell us something."

At the Broadgreen Hospital morgue a few miles away, as Larsen and Dewclaw continued to ponder this most vexatious of cases, a doctor carefully prised from Mrs Wallace's death grip, a single black chess piece.

In April 1931, William Herbert Wallace, husband of Julia Wallace, was sentenced to death for the Anfield Murder. The verdict was quashed the following month, following the first ever post-sentencing re-examination of evidence in UK legal history. The case continues to confound.

THE CAT AND THE CAKE TIN

"We have built a town, my good man. My oldest friend. My most trusted business associate. Henry William Ferdinand Bolckow." John emphasised the names as he spoke them. "What more is there for us, than perhaps a little 'sport'?"

"And what do you propose, 'Iron John'?" replied Henry Bolckow, inspecting his Meerschaum tobacco pipe.

"Something to capture the imagination of the public, I fancy," said John. "A race." He stared from the window at the men, all of them, one way or another, his employees, shuffling to and from the docks: hoppermen, foyboaters, iron smelters, platers. The human embodiment of Teesside's new industry.

"A race? The great John Vaughan involved in tawdry publicity stunts? Quite absurd," Henry said, picking at the material that coated the arm of the chair.

"Think of it," John continued, "as fantastical as the Field of the Cloth of Gold, stretched along the great banks of the Tees."

"You are but three score and sixteen years old, my friend. What seeks to race you? One of Stephenson's infernal engines? What folly."

"Do excuse me, dear friend," John said, striding forcefully towards the pantry.

Henry Bolckow closed his eyes and inhaled a long drag of Old Judge tobacco. In his reverie he considered how he, an immigrant German, had, in partnership with John, another 'outsider,' created a township, a society, an industry, in what was now known as Middlesbrough.

Like John Vaughan, Henry Bolckow, though some years younger, was in his eighth decade, coming to the end of his working life, and making plans away from the business that had made him a wealthy man. A new house was to be built, a few miles from the Cleveland Street address where both men currently resided. A grand affair, Marton Hall would house Henry Bolckow's cherished art collection, on the outskirts of the ever-growing conurbation, from where he planned to turn much of his fortune over to benevolent causes.

John Vaughan had almost been persuaded by Henry to move there himself but felt there were many years yet left in him.

Moments later, John returned from the pantry carrying an ornately gilded metal cylinder.

"A cake tin," Henry said, questioningly, "but I have eaten."

John ignored the remark.

"Calico," he said, abruptly, and then again, much louder, "Calico. Come now."

He enthusiastically banged the cake tin like a tambourine.

"Jacky," Henry cried, using the name by which John

was best known amongst his workforce, "what is this silliness?"

At that, a small tortoiseshell cat stalked into the room.

"Here he is," John announced, "Calico Jack."

The cat stopped short of joining the two men, instead eyeballing Henry from a safe distance. He resembled, rather precisely, the piratical sort, after which, one in particular, he was named.

Over his left eye, a distinctly black patch of fur that blurred at the forehead with a golden smudge over the right. Beneath, a black 'moustache' from which protruded long grey whiskers. He looked from Henry to John, unimpressed.

John reached out with the cake tin, at which Calico Jack approached, and, to Henry's surprise, hopped into it as if it were a coracle about to set sail. The tin rattled against the hard floor, then came to rest. Calico Jack preened in the glory he perceived from stepping in to the tin.

"Come, now. What is this all about?" Henry asked.

"This magnificent beast is my pilot, and sail it shall, in this very tin," John half-explained.

"Sail?" Henry said, perplexed.

"I propose a journey, comprising two and one half miles, along the grand old Tees. A point-to-point, if you will."

"Why, don't be so absurd, fellow," Henry interrupted.

The cat glared at him, as if its ability was being challenged.

"Which points do you speak of, my good man?" Henry enquired.

"To the west, the beck outlet, at the Billingham wharf, north to the river bend, then all the way east to the ferry dock," John explained.

He took out and opened his pocket watch in one smooth movement.

"I predict, with a fair wind in Calico Jack's sails, he should safely complete the voyage in…" he pondered for a moment, "twenty-six and three quarters of a minute." He snapped the pocket watch shut with a satisfactory smile.

Henry exhaled loudly, a cloud of tobacco smoke escaping into the ether, then said, "You will put this feline to sail on the most traffic-choked watercourse in the land, for some 'bet'?"

"We can close the river for thirty minutes, perhaps one hour."

"Nonsense, my man," Henry carped. "One hour out of the working day will disrupt trade beyond any immediate repair. What *will* the people have to say of it?"

"The press men will come aboard. Think of the public attention. I shall fetch Stead, the great newspaperman. The world will know of this."

"Of what?"

"That we need bridges at both points. Trade can double, nay, treble, when we are linked on both sides of this mighty serpent."

For the first time in the conversation, Henry Bolckow gave his full attention.

Calico Jack sniffed at the edges of the cake tin, as both men repacked their pipes.

The Barker heaved himself onto the makeshift wooden jetty that groaned precariously under a crowd that spilt over the river's edge and into the water, such was its number. He wore an enormous stovepipe hat bedecked with vivid Yorkshire roses and red and white coloured streamers that matched the pin stripe of his waistcoat. Over the thunderous steam-powered roar of a nearby Robert Stevenson and Company calliope, the Barker raised to his mouth a gleaming copper speaking trumpet.

"And so, on this fifteenth day of August in the eighteen-hundred-and-sixty-seventh year of Our Lord," he began, "we shall put to sail this most remarkable beast, this buccaneering bobtail, this Bengalese Blackbeard, this seafaring Siamese, that it may pass safely over the waves of the grand River Tees."

There followed an almighty roar from the gathered crowds, of men, women, and furiously excited children. The first families of the town had turned out for this most grand of occasions: Nettleton the butcher, the grocers Honeymans and Winterschladen, the wine merchant, a fellow compatriot of Henry Bolckow, all appeared at the waterside. A roaring underground trade of amateur 'turf accountants' had sprung up over the previous weeks at news of the endeavour, which had wide huge coverage in the local and national press. Men patted their chests knowingly, over the inside pockets that held their predictions, for which at least one sporting fellow had placed the princely sum of 1 guinea, almost one week's wages, that the trip could not be made in under thirty minutes. Rumours abounded, the more absurd the better to take hold. Calico Jack had been a pirate's cat, and knew the seas; that there were cats in cake tins hidden along the route ready to be dispatched if it was necessary to 'make a switch', that a syndicate of Silton Street sewer-swillers stood to win 25 guineas each.

Following the Barker's equally colourful incantation of the rules of the competition, John Vaughan, standing proudly beside Henry Bolckow on the jetty, lifted Calico Jack from a wooden crate that sat at his feet. He held the nonplussed puss up for all to see, and to reveal that Calico Jack was wearing a specially made tricorn hat held in place by a smear of wax. He grandly unveiled the cake tin that he had shown to Henry Bolckow almost a month before, before placing it onto the calm water of the Tees. It was agreed that the clock would start the moment Calico Jack's paws touched the cake tin. To a man, timepieces were taken out and carefully primed, except for those that had been snaffled by the town's much-feared pickpockets, who on this day were fully occupied in their pursuits.

Quiet fell as Calico Jack was poured into the cake tin. The perfect silence didn't abate, until the cake tin began to drift slowly away from the jetty. A murmur rolled over the crowd, and then, as Calico Jack produced an enormous disinterested yawn, bubbled into something louder as a small wave curled beneath the cake tin and took it out towards the central channels of the river. A collective roar wrought the air, which for a brief time was clear of the smog and choke of the streamers, and the ironworks.

A light wind blew northeast towards Samphire Batts, where more people had gathered. Calico Jack turned in the tin as if to face the direction of travel, like a navigator casting around for landfall. The crowd moved with him, slowly at first, and led by screeching soot-coated urchins in newsboy caps and hobnail boots.

They bawled encouragement at Calico Jack as he approached the bend in the river that would take him towards the finish line. From the bend, the Steam Packet ferry could be seen, at anchor, its patrons lining the decks and straining through eyeglasses for a view of Calico Jack coming down the home stretch. John Vaughan strode briskly along the south bank of the river, surrounded by hangers-on and jubilant supporters.

"Where'd you get him from, Jacky?" one supporter asked.

"I bet he likes a mouse, so he does," said another, pulling a handful of rotting mice carcasses from his pocket.

John Vaughan looked at his expensive pocket watch, strung from his waistcoat on a well-polished gold chain.

A few yards behind, Henry Bolckow was conveyed along in a drayman's cart pulled by two shire horses, alongside his wife, Harriet. Children patted at the horses and offered them fistfuls of grass, and became tangled in the reins and the slow thud of the hooves.

A light rain began to fall as Calico Jack twitched his nose and pawed his whiskers.

"He's waving," screamed one wag, causing the crowd to return the gesture.

"He's pointing at the line," someone else shouted.

Then drama, as an eastbound wave lifted the cake tin high in the air. Calico Jack was a sky pilot now. He stayed calm but the bookmakers cheered as he seemed to move up river, and further away from the finish line.

"Fancy a cake tin, such as that," one woman crowed, to no one in particular.

A wave of relief dampened the trepidation caused by the jolt and Calico Jack ploughed on into what was now turning into a headwind. He shook his head and blew off the sea fret that had begun to settle on his fur.

He was around 100 yards from the Steam Packet ferry, now, which floated stock still with nary a rise or drop at its waterline. A strong westerly gust of wind came over the cake tin and blew Calico Jack's tricorn hat overboard. He looked up at first, then left and right over both sides of the cake tin.

"The hat!" one woman screamed. "The hat." She looked fit to faint at the development.

Calico Jack returned to the job in hand as the cake tin arrowed towards the ferry. Beyond it lay the finish line, with no more than 300 yards to go.

John Vaughan looked calm, confident, as he strode on. Even the famously taciturn Bolckow looked to be enjoying himself.

A small boy aboard the ferry had worked himself into a frenzy at the occasion and frantically swung a wooden ratchet rattle, the kind normally reserved for raising the alarm. The head of the gragger spun and spun as the gearwheel clicked continuously, to the annoyance of the other passengers who had descended upon that part of the deck.

"Here comes Calico Jack," cried the boy, hardly heard over the din of the rattle.

The cake tin swept beneath the boat, the boy leaning over the rails, all the more to see Calico Jack. The rattle, still spinning, flew from the boy's grip and plummeted towards the water. Again, the crowds fell silent at the suspense as the rattle clattered the edge of the cake tin, throwing Calico Jack skyward once more. His body arched as he splayed out all four limbs at the top of his flying arc and plunged into the water.

John Vaughan forced his way to the front of the crowds at the river's edge, looking, for the first time, dismayed. The boy's parents tore him away from the deck rail and looked over the side. Calico Jack was nowhere to be seen. There remained only the cake tin, still on course. It had popped from the depths, Jackless.

The onlookers gulped as a whole. Men fingered their betting cards. Bookmakers crowed. Henry Bolckow stood up in his now stationary dray cart. The atmosphere has turned suddenly funereal. For several seconds no one spoke. Not even whisper. People looked to one another, expressionless.

Quietly, a jet of bubbles rose to the water's surface, followed by a blur of colour in the shape of Calico Jack as he burst from beneath like a Kraken. He soared again, a foot in the air, maybe more, somehow, and landed straight back in the cake tin.

Delirium on the river bank. Children tore at their hair in excitement, while others rolled around in the dirt. Bookmakers began to pack up their satchels and run for the hills.

Henry Bolckow even reverted to his native German. "Es läuft bei dir," he shouted. *'You're going to make it.'*

Hats flew into the air as Calico Jack bore down on the finish line, like a kingfisher swooping on its prey. The wash caused by the movement of the ferry passengers racing across the deck in one huge oleaginous shape thundered on behind the cake tin, which once again took flight, this time crossing the line, with no less than two feet of fresh air between Calico Jack and the water.

John Vaughan took a final look at his pocket watch, and closed the engraved lid.

"Did you win, Jacky?" one boy to his side cried, pulling at John Vaughan's breeches.

John Vaughan said nothing in reply. He turned to wave at Henry Bolckow as he returned his watch to his breast pocket, alongside the draughtsman's drawings for a bridge that would span the Tees.

THE BERGSTROM CASE

"You folks here on business?" the cab driver asked, leaning back over his seat and taking his eyes off Fremont Street for longer than I cared for. "Y'all got your suits on, and your briefcases, right there, huh?"

I looked across at Mr Bergstrom, calmly sitting beside me, his suitcase resting squarely on his lap. He didn't respond.

"I can hit you guys up if you need to let off steam, after your conference, or whatever the hell you guys are here for," the driver continued. He turned his eyes back to the road but glanced in the rear view mirror at me and continued talking. "I see you Limeys come into town all the time, all smart like you're Prince Charles, huh, then a few days later I'm taking you back to the airport and you owe like $300 to a call girl, and your necktie's tied around your head like goddamned Rambo on his stag party."

I smiled and patted my suitcase, rested across my knees just like Mr Bergstrom's.

"I drop you right outside the place, huh?" the driver said, veering across oncoming traffic and coming to a halt outside Binion's Horseshoe Casino. "Ol' Benny's place, huh?" he said, leaning over his steering wheel.

I handed over the fare, and a substantial tip.

"Holy shit, maybe you *are* Prince Charles," he said, folding away the note quickly.

Mr Bergstrom stepped out into the traffic without even looking, a gambler down to his bootstraps. He would take a chance on anything. I straightened my tie and strode towards the corner entrance of the casino, in step with Mr Bergstrom. The valet parking crew ogled the streetwalkers and tourist women with equal interest. A few whistles pierced the desert air, then fell away under the clip-clop of stilettoes and heavily-accented rebuttals.

A greeter approached us as we stepped onto the patterned carpet of the lobby.

"Hi, I'm Tiffany. Welcome to Binion's," she started.

Her teeth sparkled as she looked Mr Bergstrom up and down. He looked straight past her at the glass cage behind, inside which lay $1,000,000 in $10,000 bills. Or so Benny Binion himself, claimed. It looked like new money to me, and I know a big stack of cash when I see it. Whatever, it was world famous, and drew in punters for photo opportunities from all over the world.

"Where you guys from? Lemme guess... East coast, right? Hey, I'm just fooling with ya. Everyone's welcome at the Horseshoe," she said. She looked around, then leaned in and quietly said, "Except Boise State fans. Hey, I'm just joking with you guys."

I smiled. I wasn't sure what the hell she was talking about. Some sort of sporting rivalry, presumably.

"So, what are you guys looking for this evening?" she enquired.

"Myself and my associate are here to see Mr Binion," I said.

Her expression quickly changed. "Well, Mr Binion's a very busy man. I'm sure if he'd arranged to meet you guys he would've told me. Maybe you fellas got yourselves mixed up. Now, let's get you guys fixed with a drink, and out on the floor." She pondered for a moment, "You're English, right? The accent… I know it."

"Mr Binion is not expecting us. However, I'm confident a man with $1,000,000 in cash lying around his hotel lobby would be interested in what I, we, have to say," I explained, gesturing towards Mr Bergstrom.

"Well, Sir… I… I…" she stuttered, "he doesn't like to be disturbed most times."

I lightly touched her arm with my free hand and leaned into her ear.

"Tiffany," I said, "if a bunch of guys burst in here right now, armed with guns, and set about that glass box right behind us, then sauntered out with $1,000,000 stuffed in their pants, or as I suppose it to be, closer to $100,000 but cleverly stacked, they'll have missed a trick. They could have saved themselves a lot of hassle by simply demanding Mr Bergstrom's briefcase, instead. I can assure you the contents within are worth considerably more."

Tiffany began to turn, looking across the gaming floor for assistance.

"Tiffany" I said, "*you* are the most important person in this casino, right now. The first point of contact for the 5-cent one armed bandit tugger, to the cash-rich whales looking to go big. *You* make it happen. Without *you*, folks can barely get a foot in the door. It may well be Mr Binion's name over the door, but *you* are the most important person in the building right now. Don't let anybody tell you otherwise."

She looked startled. I could tell that no one had ever impressed upon her the importance of front-of-house staff in the world of big business, especially in the leisure industry. My appeal to her vanity, which was wholly sincere, seemed to work, and she waved over a man in a tuxedo, one of the pit bosses, who was watching carefully over a lacklustre roulette game nearby.

"If you fellas turn out to be all hat and no cattle, I'll run you outta town myself," Benny Binion said, the outline of his gun holster straining against the inside of his sports coat as he settled into the reassuring comfort of his oak-panelled office. His avuncular manner belied his fierce reputation and recidivist past. "Tiffany tells me you fellas are here to gamble. Well, get the hell on the floor and start playing, whydontcha?"

Mr Bergstrom laid his briefcase carefully on the desk, the clasps facing away from him.

He released them and slowly opened the case.

"$777,000," I said. "My associate wishes to stake all at your craps tables. A Don't Pass bet. One roll of the dice. It will be, of course, his first bet at this particular establishment, in keeping with your offer to honour any first bet, regardless of size."

Benny didn't even blink.

"I'll need to count up first," he said, reaching for the desk phone, "and make arrangements with the press boys, y'all understand?"

I opened my own empty suitcase, which we intended to stack the winnings in, in the same manner.

"He wishes to bet now, Mr Binion," I said, firmly.

"Whoa, now fellas, there's rules in this here Horseshoe, despite what you might have heard elsewhere. I run a square house, and have done for the damn near thirty years I been here. You better know this now: I, sure as night follows day, ain't gonna let three quarters of a million bucks stack into that empty case without getting three quarters of a million bucks worth of publicity out of it. I'll fetch the whole damn Texas Gang north for this one."

The Texas Gang were a syndicate of old school road gamblers from the Longhorn State that Benny had run with before he arrived in Las Vegas proper. They were well known back in the day. I'd heard of them, seen them around: Kilton Lane, who had supposedly lost an eye in a poker game, ex-Hollywood stunt horserider Cragg Hall and the French Baccarat wizard Millholme R'about.

"Mr Binion," I said, interlinking my fingers and resting my hands on his desk, "allow me to be frank, if I may. Mr Bergstrom doesn't give a pack mule's shit about appearing in newspapers, or those 'Texas Gang' dinosaurs. It's 1980. The last time those fellas won big, Harry Truman was president. Mr Bergstrom is as rich as a werewolf's tailor. He wants to roll, and he wants to roll now."

"Give me a day," Benny said, in a tone that suggested he wasn't used to being at the thin end of negotiations. "You fellas can't exactly walk across the street and lay your money down at The Mint or The Goose, either. Those guys'll shit through their Stetsons the minute you open that case."

"You've got an hour," I said, as Mr Bergstrom snapped shut his case.

"How about three hours?" he suggested, unconvincingly.

I glanced at Mr Bergstrom, who remained characteristically unaffected by the bargaining. He didn't move.

"One hour," I repeated, closing my empty briefcase.

"Six o'clock" he tried, pointing at the office clock.

It was just after four pm.

Mr Bergstrom gave the nod.

You're going to ask how to play craps now, aren't you, or what the hell it even is? I'm not sure myself, so I'll keep it simple-ish. Imagine a pair of gleaming dice, as red as the Devil's fingernails, studded with bone-white indices denoting numbers 1 to 6 across the six sides of each. Grab a pair, now. Take a look. Get a feel for them. Blow on them if you want, like they do in the films; it won't make any difference to me, or the dice. Now throw them across the room. Fuck it, throw them across the street. Predict the combination before they've stopped rolling. That was your 'Come Out' roll, with which you 'make your point'. Yep, that's where the term comes from. Now, get after them and add the numbers on each dice together. You've now 'made your point'. There's thirty-six possible combinations. What did you get? Snake eyes? That's a pair of ones, in Nevada parlance. Maybe you lobbed a pair of boxcars, sixes, or the doubles, the 'hard ways', did you no favours and the sugar cubes fell on odd numbers? '5-2 and fuck you' was it? It doesn't really matter. What matters is how you bet. Beginners are advised to keep it simple: doubles, odds or evens combinations, for example, although those are not great bets from the punter's point of view, and favour the House. It grows ever more complicated, but it was Mr Bergstrom's intention to bet what is called the 'Don't Pass Line' that is, to stake the entire sum on his first throw after 'making his point'.

Casinos bosses don't like disturbances. They disrupt gambling. People get distracted. Things slow down. The punters can sense it. A smashed glass or a scuffle over by the one-armed bandits draws attention away from the tables. Staff are trained to deal with it quietly and efficiently. Get the problem the hell off the gaming floor, and do it quickly. They filter through the building, these 'disturbances' carried on the air supply, and people pick up on them. There was a noticeable change in mood in the Horseshoe. Tables were moved and floor layouts were rearranged, discreetly, but noticeably to the keener eye. Bar and wait staff looked up from what they were doing, and gossiped amongst themselves. Mr Bergstrom sat quietly in the bar, refusing on multiple occasions with his customary wave, a complimentary drink, as I strolled through the gaming floor. I watched the hastily assembled press crew bustling through the front entrance equipped with Nagra tape deck equipment and pencils poised, as a flustered Tiffany corralled them into a penned off viewing area. I turned away and hovered over the Sigma Derby table as excited tourists stuffed cent after cent in the slots and jeered on their little plastic racehorses as they wobbled around the track.

Horse number 5 came up on the outside rail to win by a length. The jockey didn't look over his shoulder once.

My watch showed 5.30pm as I returned to the bar and was joined by Benny and two of his henchmen. Neither musclehead spoke, but Benny made an offer to Mr Bergstrom to carry the case, which Mr Bergstrom flatly refused. We set out towards the cashier's window where the money would be converted into chips, or, in this instance, a nickel-plated cheque-sized gold rectangle. Benny said he would honour the bet uncounted but, ever the showman, made a ceremony of taking the money to the cashiers, where counting would likely go on until after Mr Bergstrom had rolled the dice. The two goons flanked myself and Mr Bergstrom, with Benny in front of us. I looked across and sized them up. One of them had shoulders like door lintels. They arrived a few moments before the rest of him. His body didn't have the heft to turn them. His colleague had the sort of face you used to see ringside at the prizefights back in the 1950s. He was ugly, but it suited him. Benny had changed into tie and shirtsleeves. No pistol this time, at least not around his chest. It was not a good look for the shiny new age of casino gambling that he had helped usher in. It was probably jammed in his sock instead. The reporters had crowded the table, but Benny had warned them... no disturbances and absolutely *no* filming or sound recording. They all licked their pencil tips in unison as the gold tablet was presented to Mr Bergstrom beneath a silver cloche carried by a specially selected waitress. Her lips were wet and her eyes glassy as she held out the cloche and purred at Mr Bergstrom. He didn't flinch.

Despite Mr Bergstrom's insistence upon no fanfare, Benny gave a brief speech that drew the crowd in closer. There was around a hundred and fifty people set behind the cordon a few feet from the table, and inside: myself, Mr Bergstrom, Benny, the two goons, the waitress and the table staff, comprising two dealers, a boxman and a stickman.

"You folks gonna see the biggest show in town right here at the Horseshoe tonight," Benny announced. "This gentleman is about to stake $777,000 on a roll of the dice." The crowd gasped and the press pack scribbled frantically. "*The* biggest gamble this town has ever seen. Forget the D, and the Golden Nugget, and those $10 limit crapshooters at the north end of the Strip..."

This stoked the crowd and they cheered loudly and clinked glasses. "Binions is where the big boys bounce..."

The crowd were whipped up further now, but Mr Bergstrom remained as calm as ever as he was presented with five dice to inspect, from which he would select a pair. He barely gave them a glance, before giving the nod, and the unwanted trio of dice were put aside by the boxman.

"Ladies and gentlemen," Benny bellowed, "in a moment, Mr Bergstrom will now throw to make his point."

For added drama he gave a thankfully brief, but no less dramatic overview of the rules.

"Both dice *must* strike the end of the table," he bellowed, rapping a fist against the wood panelling of the table.

The reporters grew restless.

"Move it along, Benny, will ya?" one of them yelled, to laughter from his peers.

"Mr Bergstrom…" Benny said, ushering him forward.

Mr Bergstrom scattered the dice with all the insouciance of someone feeding garden birds. They arced towards the far end of the table, before lightly kissing the baize simultaneously, suggesting a carefully weighted throw. They tumbled back only slightly, side by side, and settled on a total of 6.

He carefully placed the plaque on the Don't Pass line, thus indicating that, after making his point, a 2 or a 3 would double his money, and a 12 would tie with the House, meaning Mr Bergstrom kept his money. Anything else and we were walking out of there with two empty suitcases. This then was the 'money' throw.

I didn't see Mr Bergstrom after that fateful evening in Las Vegas. As we left the Horseshoe on that balmy, midweek, mint julep kind of evening, he reached inside his jacket pocket, removed a brown envelope, and handed it to me. It contained my notice of employment, and all monies pertaining to expenses and notice period in the form of a banker's cheque. I was not surprised, or disappointed. I knew how he operated. By the time I had looked up from reading the letter of notice, he had already slipped amongst the revellers and into the desert night, as I hovered on Fremont Street, a single suitcase beside me on the sidewalk. You might think a fella with $777,000 to lose wouldn't be too concerned about whether he won or not, especially knowing Mr Bergstrom as I did, and from what you have learnt here today of his general demeanour. He was perhaps the most introverted man I have ever known, his behavioural patterns in line with what would now be considered to be associated with autism. How I came to be in his employ forty years ago is a story for another time. He was also one of the most generous men I have encountered. The banker's cheque he handed me included a bonus so substantial as to allow me to live as a man of leisure for several years after.

I was back in England, and my hometown, by 1984, working as, of all things, a croupier, in the Dragonara Hotel on Fry Street. One night a couple of Canadian tourists stopped by. We exchanged small talk, as was customary, as they laid out some small bets at the tables, before eventually retiring to the bar. Much later, as we were closing up for the night, one of the barmen handed me a newspaper.

"Thought you might be interested in this," he said, "what with you working in America before. Those Yanks left it behind."

"Er... yeah, ta. I'll have look at that," I said.

I poured myself my usual end-of-shift Old Fashioned and straightened out the newspaper. The front page was still analysing Ronald Reagan's landslide election victory of the previous week. There was some confected outrage about a new horror film, A Nightmare On Elm Street, that had been recently released, and Wild Again had won the inaugural Breeders Cup at Hollywood Park, at 33-1.

Amongst all this, somewhere towards the back pages, was a short article concerning a certain William Bergstrom, who a few days before, on November 16th, had entered Binion's Horseshoe with a suitcase full of cash, $550,000 apparently, a sack of gold krugerrands and a wad of cashier's cheques. The sum total of his war chest exceeded well over $1,000,000, according to the newspaper report. It did not explain how Mr Bergstrom had communicated his intention to bet, once again, on the Don't Pass line, without my assistance, but a 7 was rolled on the 'Come Out' throw and the whole lot went straight into Ol' Benny's satchel.

Postscript: On February 4th 1985, William Bergstrom committed suicide by overdose. He was 'in credit' to the tune of over $500,000.